THE RAILWAY DOG

Published by Brolga Publishing Pty Ltd
PO Box 12544 A'Beckett St Melbourne Australia 8006
ABN 46 063 962 443
email: sales@brolgapublishing.com.au
web: www.brolgapublishing.com.au

All rights reserved. No part of this publication may be reproduced, stored in a retrieval system or transmitted in any form or by any means electronic, mechanical, photocopying, recording or otherwise without prior permission from the publisher.

First printed in 2010
Copyright 2016 © Olwyn Parker

Information can be found in National Library of Australia Catalogue-in-Publication database.

    Parker, Olwyn.
    Bob the railway dog
    9781925367461 (pbk.)

Printed in China
Cover design by David Khan
Cover photographs courtesy of State Library of South Australia
Typesetting by Takiri Nia

THE RAILWAY DOG
The true story of an Australian outback dog

Olwyn M Parker

For Chrissie and Tilly xxx
For Nan
And, of course,
For Bob x

CONTENTS

Foreword	IX
Prologue	XI
Chapter One – *September 1884*	1
Chapter Two – *November 1884*	9
Chapter Three – *March 1885*	17
Chapter Four – *August 1888*	25
Chapter Five – *January 1889*	35
Chapter Six – *March 1889*	43
Chapter Seven – *June 1889*	51
Chapter Eight – *December 31 1891*	55
Chapter Nine – *October 1892*	61
Chapter Ten – *April 1893*	73
Chapter Eleven – *February 1894*	79
Chapter Twelve – *August 1895*	89
Acknowledgements	97
Bibliography	99
About the author	101

FOREWORD

This story, based on actual events, is about a dog called Bob, whose love of the trains took him to all corners of South Australia (and sometimes beyond) in the late 1800's. Bob became something of a legend. All the railway men knew him and kept an eye out for him – most would even share their lunches with him. Bob's registration was always kept up to date, and a special brass plate was engraved for his collar, which read, 'Stop me not, but let me jog, for I am Bob the driver's dog'. This wonderful piece of history can be found on display at the National Railway Museum in Port Adelaide. The towns that feature in this book, Terowie and Peterborough, are still very much alive, and well worth a visit. The Terowie Museum and the Hindmarsh Historical Society Museum display the only known paintings of Bob the Railway Dog. At the time this story is set, Peterborough was actually named 'Petersburg' (this being changed during WW1) but I have used the name it goes by today for ease of reading, and geographical familiarity.

PROLOGUE

The tired and dirty brown dog sat quietly in the crowded stock car, rocking back and forward with the swaying movement of the train. It had been a long, hot and seemingly endless journey.

His eyes were half closed and mucky with dust, and he huffed and puffed laboriously in the afternoon heat, a small pink tongue and strangely crooked teeth visible through the large clumps of matted fur around his face.

The dog was nameless and homeless, as no-one had ever cared enough to offer him either.

After many hours of clickety-clacking along in the hot and cramped sheep van, the huge chugging train finally began to slow down as the journey neared its end – and for that the little fellow was highly relieved, as not only was he very thirsty, but pressing in around him on all sides was a tight and jostling crowd of lively, half-wild dogs.

Excited and ill mannered, they had spent the entire trip jumping, barking and fighting, with tongues lolling, hackles up and eyes rolling. They were a very loud and rowdy bunch, and as travelling companions, left much to be desired.

As the train rattled and hissed into Terowie Station, the dog stood up and pushed his way through the whirling mass of teeth and fur, trying to reach a breath or two of fresh air.

Peering hopefully through the bars of the wagon, he could see a great open plain, still hazy in the last of the day's heat. Bleached tussocks of grass and low scrubby trees dotted the baked golden earth and, far in the distance, low hills of swirling brown velvet edged every horizon. A blustery wind spiralled dust along the ground and up onto the platform, carrying with it the scent of far-off sheep and kangaroos.

The dog stopped panting, and gazed at these new surrounds in amazement. Being a city dog, he had always assumed that the pavements and tall buildings were the whole world. Why, just this time last week he had been living off his wits on the hard streets and enjoying many thrilling adventures – a few of which involved narrow escapes from 'The Law' (otherwise known as the Council Dog Catcher). The only real blot in his carefree existence was the horrible feeling of being hungry all the time – his stomach was always rumbling and gurgling, and his thoughts were kept constantly busy with elaborate plans of how and where he might scrounge his next meal. The cruel irony was that even this, his largest of problems, had been well on the way to being solved, as he'd lately been nurturing a steady friendship with Mr Evans, owner of the largest butcher shop on Hindley Street, and a very handy chap to know.

The scruffy brown dog could often be found sitting in the alley behind the shop, waiting for scraps and leftovers from this kind-hearted and most excellent man. On one particularly memorable afternoon, Mr Evans had presented the hungry waif with a lamb shank big enough to keep him busy for a couple of days. Aaaaah! Sweet memories!

The dog's mouth watered at the thought of that shank, but the rumbling of his stomach soon brought him back to grim reality – the hot, dusty sheep van. Where was this place? What was going to happen to him?

He tried to ignore the other dogs – they held no interest for him. He had always been a friendly and well-mannered fellow, but life on the street was easier if he kept to himself and went his own way. Even packed into this carriage with two hundred other strays pressed in around him, the brown dog was still very much alone.

He thought about that day last week which had changed his life forever. It was Sunday, and the butcher shop was closed. He had decided to try a few of his old haunts in search of a meal – and it was as quick as that. One minute he was rummaging about in old Mrs Johnson's rubbish bin, and the next, a huge net had descended over the top of him, and he was well and truly caught! 'Aahaaa!' shouted the Dog Catcher, 'Got you at last, you little bugger!'

There was no escape this time, and the poor little chap knew it. Resigned to his fate, he didn't growl or try to bite, and bravely let himself be lifted up into the back of the van without making too much of a fuss.

All sorts of frightening images of his possible fate had churned through the dog's mind on that awful trip in the van, but surprisingly, life at the City Kennels had turned out to be not so bad after all. The food was good; he had a warm bed, and plenty of interesting company. The only thing he didn't have was that which was most important to him – his freedom.

After being locked in at the kennels for a week, one

morning he and about twenty other inmates were suddenly all packed up and transported out to the Adelaide city rail yards, where they joined two hundred other stray dogs being loaded onto a huge train.

The long trip to Terowie that followed was hot and dusty and uncomfortable, and as the train finally rumbled slowly into the station, they were all feeling quite miserable.

Staring out at the busy scene unfolding on the platform, the dog's bewildered gaze fell upon a man who stood apart from the gathering crowd. He was very tall and lanky, and wore a dark blue shirt with brown buttons and sleeves rolled up above his elbows. He had wrinkles around his eyes – probably not from too much laughing, he looked too serene for that – but maybe the effects of time and weather on his skin had softened him somehow.

The Man had brown hair, thick and straight, and brushed neatly off his forehead. A few grey hairs made him look a little older than he really was. The brown dog looked at the man with a yearning he didn't quite understand, but all of a sudden he did know that he desperately wanted The Man to notice him

There were a lot of people standing about on the platform, all mostly looking in at all the dogs, and chatting amongst themselves. An old porter hurrying past stopped to talk with The Man, and then they both turned and looked at the carriage where the little dog was sitting – had they seen him? He was sure the men had been looking straight at him.

After a while the porter moved on – leaving the man with the kind, weathered face standing alone again, his arms folded once more across his chest.

The dog stared, willing him to look – sensing perhaps,

a chance of rescue. He stood up against the bars, poking his face out between them for a gulp of fresh air, his shiny black nose twitching with all the new and exciting smells that came in on the breeze.

The Man had certainly noticed him now. Their eyes met, and held. It was all or nothing at this point, and the dog knew it – so he let go with an ear-splitting, attention grabbing bark, followed by his most brilliant and cheeriest smile – crooked teeth and all!

The man stood up straight, came up close to the side of the carriage, and smiled right back at him.

Yes, he'd been noticed all right. Very much so.

CHAPTER ONE
SEPTEMBER 1884

The packed and barking cargo of the 5.20 Special from Adelaide was unusual enough to have brought several of the local townsfolk out to the station platform for a closer look.

Of course, the railway men and their families who lived in Terowie were well used to seeing all manner of livestock coming and going, but two hundred dogs certainly raised a few eyebrows.

William Ferry's keen eye squinted into the evening sun as he surveyed the crowded carriages. Yowling, yipping dogs of all sizes, shapes and colours were jostling for position against the rails of the stock cars.

Will noticed his friend Harold Robbins, a porter from Peterborough, hurrying down the platform, his arms full of boxes. Harold was due for retirement in a couple of years, and was already telling anyone who'd listen about his plans to breed Suffolk sheep on a small selection out near Riverton.

The men had long ago learned not to mention sheep in front of Harold – his ability to wax lyrical for hours on the subject had them all very careful to avoid mentioning the woolly creatures at all costs.

Luckily, the subject Will wanted to discuss had nothing to do with sheep, so he felt fairly safe stopping Harold for a chat.

The deepening red and orange sunset cast wide streaks of colour across the sky, shadowing the jovial face of his old friend.

'Evenin' Harold,' he called. 'Hey, what's the story with all these dogs?'

The constant barking and yodelling from the sheep vans had by this time reached fever pitch.

Harold gave him a wide grin, showing at least three missing teeth. 'Them's the rabbiters up from Adelaide, Will, they'll be goin' on up to Carrieton, an' then out to the gangs wi' Walt Tisdale,' he shouted over the din. 'Gawd blimey, they make a bloody racket mate, don't they?'

William had heard about this new plan to overcome the rabbits. They had reached such huge numbers throughout the mid-north that entire crops were being destroyed, and fields ruined with their burrows.

To try to save the farmers' livelihoods, the government had to think of ways to destroy the rabbits, and one of these was to hunt them down with teams of dogs. As many waifs and strays as could be found were collected from the council kennels throughout Adelaide, taken by train up to Carrieton, and from there sent out with the rabbiting gangs throughout the mid-north.

Nearing the end of their long journey, the train had stopped in Terowie to take on water.

As soon as the great engine pulled in, it was all systems go for the station and its crew.

Busy men pushing handcarts hurried up and down the

platform; crates and boxes were quickly unloaded; there was shouting and bustle and whistles blowing, passengers clutching suitcases, clouds of white steam swirling across the platform – and all the while that glorious Australian sunset was bathing the land in red and pink and gold.

Leaning up against a disused luggage cart, his arms folded against his chest, Will had been watching the refitted sheep carriage with great interest – for something there had caught his attention.

Sitting quietly amidst all the hullabaloo was a shaggy, and very dirty, brown dog – just one of the crowd, but with a look in his eyes Will found hard to turn away from.

'Now there's a grand little chap!' he thought, going closer to the carriage for a better look.

The bright little face peered at him through the bars – ignoring the churning, revolving mass of unruly dogs pressed in around him, he stared straight at Will, panting loudly, and gave him the full once-over!

Now, Will Ferry was a railway man too. A tall, quiet man, he was known for being economical with words, but all the men respected his calm, easygoing nature, and they knew he could be relied upon in any crisis. He was thought to be about fifty, but probably looked a bit older than he really was. William was a hard worker and a caring husband, and his wife Mary loved him dearly, as he did her. Working long days, and sometimes being away overnight, meant leaving Mary alone in their cottage for much of the time. Terowie was a good little town, and she was well used to the country life – but William had had it in the back of his mind for quite a while now to find a decent, hearth warming companion for her. This, he thought, could be fate knocking on his door.

Walt Tisdale, the head man of the rabbiting gang, appeared at this moment with a water bucket for the dogs, and William seized his opportunity.

'Evenin' Walt' he said, 'I'm lookin' at your dogs an' thinkin' of makin' a pet out of one of 'em for the missus.'

The younger man looked at Will, aghast. 'Aw Will. Don't bother mate – they's a wild an' raggy bunch – good for huntin' an' not much else I reckon! Joe Brady down in Hallett's got some real nice puppies; one of those'd be jus' the thing for yer.'

William was silent. Walt was probably right – after all, these dogs were all of unknown heritage and character – it was just that the odd little dog had somehow taken his fancy.

He turned back to the carriage – yes, the dog was still there – panting and staring.

Lord! Was it actually smiling? Just look at those teeth!

Will's mind was made up. 'Walt, I'll give yer five bob for that brown raggy one at the front,' he said, rummaging in his pockets for the money.

'Okay mate, it's up ter you – hang on a sec!' With that, Walt disappeared around the back of the carriage, returning a few minutes later and thrusting the dog into Will's arms.

'Good luck with 'im mate!' Walt teased, hurrying back to his charges.

Alone on the platform, his heart racing a little at the commitment he'd just made, Will lifted the bristly chin and looked into the eyes of his new pet. Dog and man regarded each other silently.

'Well, I've gone an' done it now,' he thought, walking slowly down the road towards home with the furry bundle lying quietly in his arms. 'An' the little chap needs a name – I know!' He held the dog out at arms length and had a good long look at him, just to be sure. 'Yep – you cost me five bob, so that'll be your name – Bob!'

The lights of their little cottage were shining out a welcome as William turned in at the gate. Now that he was home he was feeling slightly nervous as to what Mary would say about his impulsive purchase – but as he looked down at the friendly brown eyes peering interestedly back at him through the straggly fringe, he somehow knew that everything would be alright.

As it was, there had been no need to worry – Mary Ferry loved Bob on sight. 'Oh my Lord! Will Ferry, what have you been up to!' she scolded, hands on hips and trying to look severe.

Mary was one of those lovely, caring, community-minded ladies who are the mainstay of Australia's country towns. She had three weekday dresses, all in various shades of blue (her favourite colour) and a navy and cream plaid for Sunday best. She was renowned for her feather-light scones, and was always willing to help those friends and neighbours less fortunate. Her hair, which was usually tied back in a loose bun, held a few streaks of grey, but she had a smile for everyone she met, and a kindness of spirit which kept her young.

William handed the dusty, slightly smelly little dog over to Mary's capable care – explanations would come later.

Shaking her head at the state of the raggy bundle, her motherly instincts fully roused, Mary carried Bob off in the direction of the wash house – no doubt for immediate dousing in large amounts of warm soapy water, followed by a large and hearty meal.

Bob had never known such loving care. Later that evening,

his coat clean and brushed and his stomach full to bursting, he had been put to bed in a large wooden box lined with a woolly blanket.

Poor Bob, he didn't even know what a blanket was. Was he dreaming?

The events of the last few days flashed through his mind – a series of pictures and voices and feelings that almost didn't seem real now that he had finally arrived in such a safe place. As the tension in his little body slipped away, Bob drifted off into the first really peaceful sleep he'd had in a very long time.

For the next three days and nights, Bob slept soundly in the box by the stove. He was completely exhausted, and would only wake when Mary put a steaming bowl down on the floor for his dinner each night. He would stagger up to eat, and then flop back into the box, snoring, and sometimes whimpering. William was starting to wonder if Bob would ever wake up, but he didn't say anything, even though he was getting a little worried.

'What the poor little chap must've been through.' He thought, shaking his head.

And so life went on as usual around the box, and Bob slept through it all.

Every now and then, Mary would stop her chores, go over to the box, and lightly stroke the soft brown head. Bob's tail would wag softly at the gentle touch, but still he did not wake.

He had many vivid dreams over those days and nights of sleep – most of them about the strange new world he had seen since leaving Adelaide.

This wide, strangely coloured landscape was unknown to

him – all he had known up until now were the hard city streets and sore feet, tall grey buildings, and crowds of people all too busy to notice or care about him. He was usually cold at night, and he was always hungry.

But now! Now he could see the sky!

He could feel the strangeness and loneliness of the country. He could smell sheep, and hear the birds – so many different kinds. He could hear the kind voices of William and Mary, and feel the warmth and safety of his new home.

Finally, early on the morning of the third day, Bob woke up.

It took him a few moments to remember where he was.

He looked around the kitchen. A large wooden table stood in the middle of the room, and a comfy, overstuffed chair with flowery cushions sat on the other side of the warm Aga stove. The steady tick-tocking of Mary's prized mantle clock was the only sound. Tiny particles of dust danced in the sunbeams streaming through the window. His box was comfortable and warm. He felt safe, and his stomach was full.

Today was a great day – the beginning of Bob's new life – and if only he'd known it, many exciting adventures to come!

CHAPTER TWO
NOVEMBER 1884

It was a cold, clear morning just before dawn. The front gate clicked shut behind William as he headed off down Main Street towards the railway station, for another long trip down to Adelaide and back. Mary had fixed a lunch pail for him as he would be gone all day.

Whistling softly as he walked, Will shivered a little as his breath turned to steam in the icy air. The first soft shades of morning were edging the horizon, but above him a million stars still glittered brightly in the clear black sky.

Turning into Besanko Street, the lights of the station up ahead, Will suddenly sensed a presence at his heel, and, turning to look over his shoulder, found Bob trotting quietly along behind him.

The game was up, and the little dog grinned at him guiltily, all his crooked teeth on show.

'Aw Bob!' Will said crossly, 'What to do now? I'll be late if I 'ave to take you 'ome.'

William was quite exasperated with Bob. He knew the dog was fretting at home – Mary had told him of the crying and scrabbling at the door after he left for work each day, and obviously this morning Bob had escaped while Mary wasn't looking. Will realised he didn't have many options at this stage – the dog had outsmarted him.

'Well laddie – looks like you'll 'ave to come along wi' me after all,' Will said resignedly to the cheery little face, 'Come on then!'

Bob, thus released of all guilt from his misdemeanour, barked excitedly and ran on ahead, 'As if 'e already knows where we're going,' thought Will, watching the happy little dog running ahead in the dim light, ears back and tail waving – he was off on an adventure!

Far in the distance, a lone magpie's melodic warbling echoed across the plain.

'Funny they're always the first birds awake in the mornin'.' he thought. Soon the galahs, the corellas, and those awful black crows would be up too, but the magpies were always the bell ringers of the coming day.

Smiling at the thought of those lovely 'early birds' and swinging his arms to keep warm, Will strode across the last few yards of road, and up the steps into the office at the back of the station, Bob close at his heel.

Out on the long platform, it was 'action stations' and all go! Kerosene lanterns provided enough power to illuminate the busy tableau, as the men prepared the train for it's first journey of the day.

Bob watched the scene unfold with great interest – the hustle and bustle of preparations for the day ahead were fascinating to him. Later, thinking back over the day, he would remember pictures and sounds – hissing steam, hurrying men, boxes and handcarts, whistles blowing, loud voices and laughter, and, already, a feeling of belonging.

Bob's destiny was starting to take shape.

The men stood in a circle, nudging each other and looking down at the dog. They had all heard the story of Will's purchase from the rabbiting gang, and were delighted to have the opportunity of some good-natured ribbing at Will's expense.

'Brought a friend mate?' they teased.

'Distant relative from your side of the family tree is 'e Will?'

Will rolled his eyes heavenward and shook his head.

'It's alright lads, Bob won't be any trouble.' Will's confident tone belied his anxiety, as he bent down to pat the soft brown head. 'E's a good dog, an' does as I tell 'im.'

The truth was, that Will could have sent Bob home with the Stationmaster's boy, as he was sending a note to Mary with the lad anyway (he needed to let her know of Bob's whereabouts so that she wouldn't spend the day worrying), but he felt strangely flattered that the dog was so keen to be with him, and wanted to give him a chance to prove himself.

The note for Mary duly written, and sent off quicksmart with young Ern, Will had just enough time to get the paperwork organized for today's freight to Adelaide. Luckily the trip should be fairly straightforward – a load of wheat to take down, and general supplies to bring back.

Bob sat by the open office door, looking out onto the busy platform.

When he first came up on the train to Terowie, he had been so fretful and busy trying to look brave, that he didn't really remember much of the actual train trip. But now, weeks later, with a safe home and a kind master, he was seeing everything with new eyes.

He felt the excitement, the smells, and the noise of the trains like a revelation.

Will was watching Bob with quiet amusement – his ears were swivelling in all directions, and his nose lifted high into the air, sniffing and inhaling all the exciting aromas emanating from the rail yards. Bob was in sensory overload!

'Alright lad – it's time to be off!'

With all the paperwork done, Will was ready to climb on board the train to start his day's work. Pulling the office door shut behind him, he waved at Harold, who was waiting at the end of the platform for the signal. John McDonald, the day's driver, had already primed the engine, and clouds of steam swirling around the platform enveloped the train, hiding the engine from view as they approached.

Will bent down to give Bob a pat. 'Be a good dog today, laddie – don't be scared.' And with that he picked Bob up and hoisted him aloft into the great hissing, huffing, beautiful locomotive.

Bob's destiny had arrived. The noise inside the small cabin was thunderous. Bob was thrilled to his very core! His ears were pricked, his hair stood on end, and he panted and puffed and barked as his tail waved madly at all angles.

Down on the platform, the guard blew his whistle, waved his flag – the engine gave a slight lurch, and they were off.

Will and John were laughing at Bob's antics, and Will was already getting the feeling that Bob would likely be joining him on many more trips in the future.

'Jus' like a duck ter water!' he thought, watching Bob already adjusting to his 'train legs,' and leaning into the bends. As the train huffed and puffed its way out of Terowie through the early morning light, a mob of kangaroos could be seen moving in the far distance, their sleek bodies bounding effortlessly across the plain, the sun's first gentle rays warm on their backs.

It was beautiful country this, the colours of the landscape ever changing as seasons came and went, always something new to see – the light on the distant hills, the shimmering haze of summer stretching out across the baking brown plains, and then the first flush of green as winter approached and the rains came – never enough rain of course, but that was only to be expected the further north you went.

Will and John were kept busy with the running of the great engine, and after a while Bob calmed down a bit, and settled into a corner by Will's lunch pail. He watched the goings-on around him with great interest and from his position, could see not only the workings of the inside of the train, but also a perfect view of the passing landscape from between Will's legs.

The countryside flashed past, small towns came and went, and Bob enjoyed the best day of his life. Clickety–clack, clickety-clack, clickety-clack, the endless northern miles rolled away, and before too long the golden wheat fields and far horizons were far behind them, and the beginnings of civilization were in front. Houses appeared, and roads and shops, and then all too soon they were pulling into the huge railway yards in Adelaide.

How different were Bob's circumstances on his return to the city. He had left here six weeks ago as an unwanted, hungry street urchin – and now to be here again as a confident, much-loved pet who really belonged, and had his own place in the world. Bob saw the whole world in a new light these days – he was actually getting quite cocky, Will would say! As soon as the train stopped, Bob did something unexpected. He made a huge leap down from the cabin and took off, weaving his way across the rails, and in and around other stationary carriages. Will, horrified, could do nothing but watch helplessly until the little figure had disappeared from view.

'Lord, what've I done?' he thought, 'Ten to one I'll never see the little chap again.'

Poor Will was to suffer a miserable couple of hours before the return trip to Terowie. He thought Bob might be lost forever; and how he would explain that to Mary, he just didn't know.

Bob, however, knew exactly where he was going – the streets of Adelaide were, after all, his old stamping ground.

Being a dog usually means that food is very high on the list of things to think about, so as soon as Bob had realised that the train was returning him to Adelaide, he had been thinking of his friend Mr Evans, the butcher. His faith in Will was such that he knew he wouldn't be left behind, so at the first opportunity, he was off and running through the busy rail yards, under the fence, across North Terrace, and up the hill towards Hindley Street.

Mr Evans was amazed and relieved to find Bob sitting in his old place at the back of the shop, holding his paw up for a shake, just as if he'd never been away.

'By Jingo! I thought you was gone for good, young fella!' He patted Bob's head very enthusiastically, and accepted the offered paw with a wide grin.

'Where've you been all this time matey? I didn't think we'd be seein' you again!'

Mr Evans couldn't help but notice the physical changes

in Bob, who was now, after six weeks of Mary's loving care, quite a different dog. The thin, wary little dog with the matted, scruffy coat was gone, and in his place had appeared this cheery, well fed, perfectly groomed pet, who greeted him with all the enthusiasm of a long lost friend! It didn't take Mr Evans too long to realise what had happened.

'Gawd lad – you've found a proper 'ome! Well done ol' mate!' He rubbed Bob's ears and shook his paw again, 'Just 'ang on a sec, I've got a liddle somethin' for yer!'

The old man hurried inside, and soon returned with two fat pork sausages, which he presented to Bob with a flourish. 'There you go laddie – enjoy 'em with my compliments!'

And so a happy routine began between the two old friends. Whenever Bob had an opportunity to travel down to Adelaide, he would head straight up to the little butcher shop on Hindley Street for a visit and a snack before the next train departed for Peterborough, Port Adelaide, or Broken Hill.

Back down at the Adelaide station yards, Will had not been having such a happy time. Two hours had passed, and the train was now reloaded and ready to depart for the return trip to Terowie. There was still no sign of Bob, and Will was starting to feel very worried that they would have to leave without him.

Standing high in the engine's cabin, Will waited anxiously, one hand shielding his eyes from the sun as he scanned about desperately for any sign of his wayward little dog. It was time to leave – the engine was primed, clouds of black smoke were chugging from the huge funnel – and suddenly, there was Bob!

Bouncing over the tracks, ears and tail flying, dodging and weaving around the other trains, he caught up just as they were pulling out of the station. Will climbed down to the lowest footrest.

'Come on, lad!' yelled Will, leaning down with one arm beckoning madly,

'Come on! Jump!'

Bob jumped alright. Will's sure grip caught a tight hold of his scruff, and he swung Bob up and into the cabin before either of them had a chance to think twice.

Will was red-faced and just about speechless. Bob jumped about in excitement at being up in the train again, with no idea of the worry he'd caused, or that he'd almost been left behind. John McDonald laughed as if he'd never stop, eyes watering, bent over double and dabbing at his tears with an oily hanky – he had been thoroughly entertained, and would certainly be making the most of this story when he retold it to the men on their return to Terowie.

His head clutched in his hands, Will shook his head in relief. He couldn't believe what a close call that had been, and his knees were still shaking.

Bob pressed up against his legs, tail waving uncertainly, ingratiating smile at full wattage – he knew he'd cut that a bit fine, but aaah! Those pork sausages had been well worth all the fuss.

CHAPTER THREE
MARCH 1885

Bob sat on the grassy verge at the top of Government Road, looking down upon the township of Peterborough spread out below. This was about the highest point in the district, and from here he could see where the land met the sky in every direction. It was just on dusk, and the deepening twilight cast dark shadows in the soft folds of the far-off hills. As the flaming reds and purples of the setting sun faded gently to a dim glow, the stars came out – one by one – until the vast black sky was full of glittering, shining lights.

The sky didn't look like this in Adelaide, and Bob had never connected the two as being one and the same.

After applying for a transfer almost a year ago, Will had just about given up hope as the months went by with no reply – and then all of a sudden in January, the notice had finally come through. Six weeks later he, Mary and Bob had left Terowie to move to Peterborough, a busy railway town on the northern side of the Gumbowie Hills.

Mary was delighted with the large, modern house that had come with Will's promotion to Assistant Stationmaster, and Bob had been equally excited when he discovered that the railway line actually ran right past their new front door. He could sit out on the verandah at any time of the day or night and watch the trains go by.

Bob had soon learned all the routines and schedules of Peterborough's busy railway station – after all, it was conveniently situated right next door. Everything that happened there could be heard clearly from the house; people shouting and laughing, whistles blowing and of course, those huge chugging, puffing locomotives, rumbling past the house at all hours and rattling the windows.

The station was very cosmopolitan, with a steady stream of people and goods coming and going; and there was usually a queue of buggies, carts, and a bullock wagon or two parked out the front.

It didn't take long for Bob to become well known as a 'regular' – both on the platform and around the station tearooms. The cheerful brown dog, barking excitedly as each train pulled in, and greeting the bemused passengers with his crooked grin and ever–waving tail, quickly gained a reputation as the 'meet' and 'greet' dog of Peterborough, whose enthusiasm for his job could raise a smile from even the most weary of travellers. Bob's loyalties, however were soon being pulled in two directions – as right on the other side of Hurlestone Street, was a place possibly even more exciting than the station – the rail yards. Here was a place of twenty-four hour activity, where he could go at any time and always be sure of finding good company and action aplenty.

The yards consisted of a curved row of enormous sheds, each one housing a locomotive engine. The huge 'roundhouse' with its hundreds of small windowpanes, was right next door to the accommodation building, where the men ate, and sometimes slept. In the middle of the yards was the huge turntable, enabling any engine or carriage to be brought out of the sheds, turned slowly around, and directed onto the main line. It was at the yards with the men where Bob felt as if he really belonged.

Most mornings he would trot along to work with Will, bright eyed and eager, happy to go anywhere as long as it involved being in or near the trains. It was taken for granted now that Bob would travel with Will wherever he went, although Will's journeys had been much less frequent since his promotion.

So life quickly settled into a nice routine, and all was peaceful on both the home and work fronts until one day, about a month after their arrival in Peterborough, a fateful telegraph arrived that threw the whole station crew into a state of unholy dread.

William, who had only left for work two hours earlier, came rushing home in a panic. He was in such a state that he didn't even notice the delicious aromas of Mary's baking day filling the peaceful sunlit kitchen. Red faced and out of breath, he charged through the house, pulling off his dirty clothes as he went and leaving a trail of the discarded garments all the way up the passage.

As he was generally a very calm and quiet man, Mary knew something was definitely amiss as she followed him worriedly into the bedroom.

'Will dear, whatever's the matter – have you hurt yourself? Are you ill?'

'I need me spare uniform,' he shouted from the depths of the wardrobe, 'Give us a hand will yer, Love, I'm in a real bloody hurry here!'

The news couldn't have been worse – the Commissioner was coming up from Adelaide for a surprise inspection of the station and yards. According to the telegraph just received from town, he had boarded the Northern Express at eight o'clock this morning, and would be arriving in Peterborough within the hour.

Tensions were high as the men hastened to make everything ready. The platform was hurriedly swept, uniforms brushed down, brasses polished, bookwork re-checked – the minutes ticked by much too quickly.

Will returned with only minutes to spare in a clean, freshly pressed uniform and shiny shoes. All was tidy and shipshape as the Commissioner's train pulled into the station, and Will's fingers were tightly crossed in the hope that everything would run smoothly. Any faults or problems noticed today would be Will's responsibility, and he was feeling very nervous, even though the station looked immaculate and everything was in good order. He had every reason to be apprehensive – the Commissioner was a man of fearsome reputation, who had been known to leave even the bravest of fellows quaking in their boots with his acid tongue and withering stare. His penchant for sacking good men on the spot for even the most minor of infringements was legendary, and every station in the state lived in fear of his surprise inspections. However, as is often the case with workers' attitude to an arrogant superior, there were a few quite humorous tales doing the rounds as well – some of which depicted the haughty man in a less than flattering light.

One of the most popular of these went back to his days as Superintendent at Port Pirie Station, when he found himself responsible for unloading Jim Hartleys' grand piano – a huge hand carved monolith that the wealthy landowner had imported from England as a gift for his young wife.

It was a delicate job, but the men working that day had everything under control, fitting wide straps around the piano, and preparing to lift it out onto a large gurney. Feeling the need to assert his authority, and completely disregarding all suggestions from the experienced crew, he took over the job, ordered people about, and personally re-fitted the straps. The men could see this was a disaster waiting to happen, and told the Superintendent so in no uncertain terms. Taking offence at their insolence, he put them all on report, and persisted with the job his own way. Of course, it all went wrong at the crucial moment, and they could do nothing but watch helplessly as the piano tipped slowly sideways in mid-air before falling ten feet down onto the tracks with an almighty thunderous crash!

As the story goes, there was one full minute of silence, broken only by the loud echoing twang of the shattered keys. As the men stood looking down in horror at the ruined piano, the then Superintendent's face flushed from bright red to a deep throbbing purple as his fury and embarrassment exploded! He was a great one for swearing, and never used the same word twice. Everyone watched, speechless, as he stalked the entire length of the train and back again, with a different swear word for every carriage he passed. The afternoon crew, who had arrived at work just in time to see their mortified boss being bawled out by a furious Jim Hartley, thought it a wonderful joke – the Superintendent being thoroughly disliked by most of them.

So, five years later, and with his Commissioner's badge sparkling in the winter sunshine, the great man descended the small steps onto the platform.

He was well over six feet tall, and had a stiff, military bearing which corresponded well with his immaculate uniform and shining brasses. In fact, if one was meeting him for the first time with no knowledge of his history, he would be taken for a very impressive man. Either way, the whole station crew knew that this was a very important visit – if the Commissioner went away unhappy today, he would in all likelihood make their lives miserable in the future.

Tensions were high as he made his way along the platform and up towards the front of the train. The men were all spruced and correct, standing straight and tall as he walked down the ranks checking every detail of their turnout. Everything seemed to be going well, the Commissioner smiling benignly and nodding his head as he went along the line.

Suddenly, out of the corner of his eye, Will saw movement at the far end of the platform. He paled visibly.

'Oh Lord no – not now!' he thought in a panic.

There was Bob, trotting casually up the platform towards the men – tongue lolling, eyes bright with expectation – sure of his welcome. The Commissioner hadn't noticed the dog yet, and Will didn't intend to invite disaster by letting Bob introduce himself.

Will hissed out of the corner of his mouth to Harold, who was standing straight and correct beside him, 'Quick Harold, distract 'im for God's sake!'

By this time, Bob had drawn level with the front of the train and, evidently making up his mind to get in early (so to speak) had jumped up into the engine compartment to await his next ride out of town.

Much to Will's relief, Bob was now momentarily hidden

from view – but he knew that as the great man drew level with the cabin, he would hardly fail to notice the shaggy, smiling dog sitting upright in the drivers seat, and then there would be hell to pay. For all of them.

With no time left to come up with a decent plan, and the Commissioner almost upon them, Will and Harold had to think fast! Three more steps and the interior of the cabin would be visible – one, two – and then good old Harold stepped in to save the day.

He turned to the Commissioner and drew him a few steps back down the platform, leaning out over the rails and pointing out some intricacy of the line gauges.

Without hesitation, Will leaned into the cabin, scooped Bob up in his arms and then with one big swing, hoisted him up onto the coal tender behind the engine. He nearly didn't make it all the way, and there was a bit of scrabbling as Will pushed the furry bottom from behind, but so far so good – by some miracle they hadn't been seen.

'Bob!' he hissed 'Stay!'

Bob looked down at Will, his head cocked quizzically to one side,

'Bob – stay!'

He didn't really understand the words, but Will's tone left no room for doubt. For the moment Bob was hidden from view and Will, his face crimson with stress, stepped back into line just as the Commissioner turned to face the train again.

Sitting quietly on top of the coal, Bob looked around with interest. This was certainly a different view of the world. He could see everything – leaves on the station roof, the tops of all the carriages stretching behind the engine like a great long snake, the far away hills – it was fantastic! A warm breeze ruffled his fur, and he felt very comfortable and at ease in his new found eyrie.

An hour later, when the inspection was over, and the Commissioner was safely installed in a comfortable room at the Peterborough Hotel, Will returned to the engine and gave a low whistle. A brown head appeared, looking down at him from high above. By the way the head was moving from side to side, Will could tell Bob's tail was wagging madly as usual.

'You right up there fella? What a good dog you are!' When Will lifted Bob down from the tender, he had no idea what he'd started – for from that day forward, Bob rarely rode anywhere else but the high, exclusive position on top of the coal pile – barking and yodelling his joy from one town to the next.

CHAPTER FOUR
AUGUST 1888

The night was clear and very cold, as is often the case in the outback, no matter what the time of year.

Bob was at home, curled up in his box by the stove, but he wasn't asleep – something was wrong. Dogs often seem to know when things are going to happen, even before they actually do, and tonight Bob was getting one of those bad feelings. He got up and started pacing around the kitchen, ears flicking back and forth and nose twitching, He felt like growling, but didn't know why – so, being a very smart dog, he thought he'd better go outside to see what was going on. He scrabbled and pushed at the back door (Mary always left the door off the latch at night, so Bob could go outside if he needed to) and let himself out into the street.

Outside, the town was dark and quiet, and the cold night air made Bob shiver.

There was no moon, but thousands of stars glittered brightly in the endless black sky. The buildings and streets were eerily illuminated in the dim blue starlight, and for a brief moment he wished so heartily for the warmth and safety of his box by the stove, he nearly turned and ran back inside.

But no! There really was something not right – was that a faint whiff of smoke? Bob's hackles went straight up again – he must go on.

Trotting up Railway terrace, Bob turned to look up Hurlestone Street towards the hospital – no, nothing there. He could hear all the usual night time sounds – the distant 'baaaing' sheep, and cicadas in the gardens. Bob was still adjusting to his new life away from the bustling, clamorous city. He had been living in the country for nearly four years, and yet still marvelled at the different smells and sounds (some of these were even now a mystery to him), the quietness at night: even the sunlight felt brighter, and more golden somehow. Bob's whole world had changed, and he had adapted to his new life as a 'country dog' with a home and family very quickly.

Passing the Peterborough Hotel, he could hear voices and laughter inside, and that peculiar smell (pipe smoke and beer, but Bob didn't know that!) hung thickly in the air out the front, making his nose twitch. Things, however, changed as he progressed further up the street – the town was dark, and appeared deserted. He shivered a little, thinking longingly again of his cosy box at home.

Most of the townsfolk had retired fairly early, closing the curtains and stoking up their fireplaces as evening settled in and dinner was made. All appeared to be calm and peaceful. It was not. Suddenly, Bob's ears pricked up and his nose twitched. Smoke! It was smoke! Not like the warming, cosy wafts from the fireplace at home, or Will's evening pipe – this was different – this was –Very Alarming.

He could see it now, flames, just small ones, were licking brightly at the window of the General Store.

Bob's hackles went up, and all his hair stood on end. He barked as loudly as he could.

He ran and barked all the way back to the Hotel, and right up to the door. Bob was very good at scrabbling at doors, so this he did – whining and scrabbling and barking, until Bert Steadman (one of Will's friends from the rail yards) opened the door, and Bob fell in a heap into the room.

'Why Bob, lad – what's the matter? It's Will Ferry's dog!' he called over his shoulder into the room behind. The voices and clinking glasses went quiet.

Bob, in a frenzy of fear and excitement, jumped and pulled at Bert's coat, ran outside, ran back, jumped again – it didn't take too long to figure out something was wrong.

'Jack! Come on mate, we'd better take a look at what's wrong wi' the dog!' he called to his friend Jack Cunningham.

Bert and Jack could have been brothers they were so much alike. Born within a week of each other on neighbouring farms, their mothers best friends, the two boys had grown up together, sharing adventures and schooldays, and now, as grown men, both working for the railways.

Bert and Jack were tall, lanky and merry-eyed – Bert's hair as dark as Jack's was fair, and both of them very honest and well-liked young men about the district.

On this particular evening, as like many others, it made sense that they would be found together, finishing a quiet beer after a long day with the ore trucks up at Broken Hill.

Once outside on the street, with Bob jumping and barking around them and trying to swing off their ankles, Jack and Bert could see immediately that Judells Store was on fire.

They ran pell mell up the road towards the shop. 'Bert!'

panted Jack, 'That cellar's full o' dynamite – if it blows, half the bloody town'll go!'

They stared at each other for a moment, the danger of the situation very clear to both. A decision was made without words being spoken.

They clambered quickly over the side fence and ran around to the back of the store. Shoulders heaved once, twice, three times on the back door – it finally gave way with a loud crack, and, kicking aside the splintered wood, they rushed inside.

At this point, the flames were confined to the front of the store, although smoke was rapidly filling the building. Bert could see straight away that the fire had too strong a hold for them to try putting it out.

'Jack! We 'ave to get the dynamite out before the flames get too close – there's no other way!'

Jack's face paled at the thought (he was really starting to wish he'd gone straight home after work tonight) but he knew Bert was right. They were committed now – there was no turning back. He nodded grimly to his friend, and crossed his fingers.

The swirling black smoke was getting thicker by the minute, and they could hear the crackling and popping of the flames – too close!

Bert set off at a run out to the well in the backyard, stripping off his shirt as he went. Frantically working the pump handle up and down, he soaked the shirt in the icy cold water, and then raced back into the store, wrapping the garment around his head and face.

Jack waited at the top of the cellar stairs. Providence had led him to a couple of lanterns on the shelf in the hallway

– hurriedly lighting them with shaking hands, he put one halfway down the steps and gave the other one to Bert.

'Orright mate,' he said grimly, 'Lets bloody do it then!'

They worked, as usual, as a perfect team.

★

Outside on the street, meanwhile, Bob had also been busy. Told firmly to 'Stay!' he had sat on the footpath for a few minutes, trying to be good, but as the fire really started to take hold of the buildings, and Bert and Jack still had not returned, he knew he couldn't wait any longer.

Running up and down the road, his head held high in the air, Bob set up a yowling and wailing such as he had never attempted before. It worked very well! Lights began appearing in windows and doorways, and other patrons of the bar gathered on the hotel's verandah.

Bert and Jack, however, were oblivious to Bob's efforts. Back inside the store, Jack waited at the top of the stairs, grabbing the boxes of dynamite as Bert brought them up, running with them out through the back door, and piling them up in the furthest corner of the back yard.

Back and forward, back and forward, puffing, sweating, wheezing and coughing in the thick smoke, staggering under the weight of the heavy boxes. All around them was heat, and blinding, choking smoke – and worst of all, their own heart-pounding fear. Any moment could be their last, but it simply had to be done – there was no turning back now.

Luckily, and all thanks to Bob, most of the town was up by now and out in the street. Horrified to see the store on fire, and unaware of Bert and Jack's efforts out the back, a desperate battle to save the building was underway. A human chain had quickly been formed, and buckets of water were being thrown through the now broken front windows and onto the roaring flames.

Thick black smoke billowed up into the night sky. Showers of sparks rained down onto the street.

Those at the front of the line could feel their faces scorching. The heat was incredible, but no-one backed away – they knew they couldn't afford to lose the store, it was too important to the town. Bucket after bucket of water was hurled into the roaring red and orange flames, and gradually the fire began to abate. A shout went out as the townsfolk (all in various hurriedly-pulled-on-clothing arrangements) could see they were winning the fight at last.

As Bert lurched out the back door with the last box of gunpowder, Jack close at his heels, the two young men felt utterly spent. Coughing up soot, and with blackened hands and faces, they carefully placed the last of the deadly powder on the pile with the rest, before collapsing, exhausted, onto the grass.

They were still there half an hour later when Horrie Judell and the local policeman arrived around the back to check on the fate of the dynamite, and found, to their horror, the two young heroes lying prone on the grass. It only took them a moment to take stock of the situation – the scene laid out before them told the tale pretty clearly.

'…and there was Will Ferry's dog, Bob,' the policeman later told his wife after arriving home in the early hours, 'sittin' between the two of 'em all concerned-like, starin' at one, then t' other, quiet as a mouse so's not to wake 'em up!'

Much later into the night, when the fire was well and truly

out, and Bert and Jack had been taken up to the hospital on the back of Horrie's dog cart, the fuss started to die down a bit and the townsfolk began heading for home and bed. There was nothing more to be done until morning.

Dawn's first gentle light revealed the full extent of the damage wrought by the deadly blaze.

The entire front of the store had been left a smouldering ruin — blackened and scorched brickwork still radiated heat, and thin wisps of smoke curled lazily into the cool morning air from piles of twisted timber and ruined stock. The good news, however, was that the rear storerooms and cellar were relatively untouched by the flames, and many of the town's valuable supplies were able to be salvaged without too much damage.

Of course, word of the dramatic events of last evening had spread quickly throughout the district, and a steady stream of concerned onlookers spent the day 'Oohing' and 'Aahing' at the smoking ruins, with some quite enjoying the disaster now that it was known the damage wasn't too severe.

Up at the hospital, Bert and Jack lay like kings in a private room, their every need attended to by a cheerful nurse called Bridget, who was very firm in making them 'Lie still and rest for 'eaven's sake!'

To make things worse, the doctor had then arrived and ordered a week of complete bed rest and plenty of strong chicken broth, brushing aside their protestations with a wave of his hand and a dire warning about the risks of getting up too soon and causing permanent damage to their already scarred lungs. After a few half-hearted protests, and feeble attempts to get up and out of bed, they soon realised that they would be quite happy to obey on this occasion, both of them feeling weak and short of breath still.

Thus resigned to their fate, Jack and Bert lay back on the soft pillows and gave themselves up to the dedicated efforts of Bridget. They were too exhausted to argue any more, and secretly relieved to just sleep.

★

Someone else greatly in need of a good rest was Bob.

Safe at home now, and curled up tight in his box, his tail thumped a little at the memory of his frightening, but also very exciting, evening.

As soon as he had seen that the townsfolk were going to be successful in extinguishing the fire, Bob had hurried around to the back of the store. He could see that Bert and Jack were lying on the ground having a sleep, which seemed a bit strange. He sniffed and pawed at them a little, but they didn't move. On top of that, they smelled awful – all smoky and scared. It made him feel nervous, but everyone else was out the front putting out the fire, so he just sat down between them to keep an eye on things, and that was how the policeman and Horrie Judell found them all later.

William and Mary had stared in blank amazement as heavy pounding on their front door in the early hours had signaled the triumphant return of Bob, cradled gently in the arms of the towns' burly policeman. Bleary-eyed and dressed in their night-attire, they had been astonished to hear of Bob's night-time escapades, and the near destruction of the general store.

Back in their bed an hour later, the little hero safely tucked up in his box in the kitchen, Mary whispered drowsily, 'We shouldn't be that surprised, Dear – after all, we've known right from the start there's somethin' special about 'im!'

★

Several weeks later, things had just about returned to normal in Peterborough. The debris from the fire had been cleared away, and work had commenced on rebuilding the shop front. Horrie said perhaps it was just as well, as now he was able to extend the front of the building and put in bigger windows, which he had been wanting to do for ages.

After making a steady recovery, Jack and Bert had been discharged after six luxurious days in the hospital's best room. They were under strict instructions from the doctor to 'take things slowly and get plenty of rest,' for at least the next two weeks.

By mutual agreement, the first stop on their way home was William and Mary's cottage. Luckily, Bob was home that morning, and as the two heroes sat at Mary's kitchen table working their way through a mountain of hot cheesy scones, Bob weaved his way around the legs of their chairs, wagging his tail, grinning, enjoying the friendly hands patting him under the table, and the furtive pieces of scone appearing like magic in front of his nose! Bert and Jack could not have been more grateful for Bob's help on that awful night, and they told Mary how lucky she was to have such a special dog. As she waved them off later from the front door step, Bob's thumping tail tickling her leg, she knew it was true.

★

A month later, Bert and Jack were invited to the Peterborough Town Hall to receive an award for their bravery. Red faced and humble, they accepted the gratitude of the town; the cheering applause as the Mayor shook their hands was deafening, and the smiling dog in the front row, oblivious to his own part in the story, was never forgotten by either of them.

CHAPTER FIVE
JANUARY 1889

The December heatwave had been unrelenting.

Five long weeks had passed with temperatures above ninety degrees, and everyone – people and animals alike – were heartily sick and tired of it. The whole district sweltered under the shimmering summer haze.

Sheep, those hardiest of animals, stood motionless in the blazing sun, their heads bowed. Some were lucky enough to find small patches of shade under the few scrubby trees and clumps of saltbush, but mostly they just waited out the long hot days as best they could.

That other mainstay of the outback farmers – the cattle – stood with their backs to the sun, swishing their long tails back and forth, back and forth, trying to fend off the constant, merciless flies.

Stoic mothers preparing for Christmas were committed to their kitchens – stoves blazing, baking pies and cakes and roast lamb for the menfolk. They wiped the sweat from their eyes, fanned the babies, and wished longingly for a cool change.

Over at the schoolhouse, teachers and students sat outside under the giant pepper trees for their lessons. Apart from the stifling heat, there weren't too many distractions – even the noisiest birds fell quiet in the heat of the day.

New Year came and went, and it just got hotter and hotter.

The paddocks and scrubby bushland were tinder dry, and the ever-present threat of fire weighed heavily on everyone's minds. Some of the older men in town rumoured a change was coming, but to most people, the heat felt never-ending.

By the second week of January, however, something was definitely in the air. On the Friday, menacing black clouds had begun to gather on the horizon, blocking out the sun and turning the blue sky to grey. A cool, gusty breeze whipped up, spiralling leaves and dust down the main street of Peterborough and out across the fields.

Bob, his head down, squinting through the stinging dust, trotted quickly down the street towards home. He had just returned from a day trip down to Adelaide on the 5.20 Special, and was hoping for a large dinner of last night's leftover roast beef. He knew there was also a large cinnamon cake in the pantry, but that was probably a bit too much to hope for.

It was already almost dark, and tension filled the air.

Bob turned in at the gate, went around to the rear of the house, and scrabbled at the back door, which swung open wide as Mary ushered him in.

'Lordy!' she exclaimed, shielding her eyes as debris from the yard blew in through the doorway. 'Looks like the change is 'ere at last!' Mary had opened all the windows, but it was still too hot for Bob to sleep in his box, so after dinner (the leftover roast beef, but no cake) he just flopped down onto the cool brick floor, panting and dozing – eyes half shut and tongue lolling, reliving the thrilling journey from which he had just returned, ears twitching each time the train's whistle blew in his dream.

By mid evening, the distant rolling thunder of the afternoon had reached the Gumbowie Hills and developed into a fierce, unrelenting storm, the consequences of which would be talked about for many years to come.

BOOOOOM! Bob's ears flicked back and forward. BOOOOOM! CRAAAACK! His eyes opened. Wide! Poor Bob woke with a jump as another enormous thunderclap exploded directly overhead. At this moment, all over Peterborough many lesser dogs than he were howling and shaking with fear. The resounding blasts filled the air and shook the house. The thunder was even louder than the roar of Bob's beloved steam engines. Great forks of lightning slashed the sky and lit up the kitchen in an eerie silver glare. Bob was not worried – he had tucked himself up in his box in the place he felt safest, and William and Mary were there with him, gazing in awe at the spectacular display through the window.

He felt no fear, as dogs often do in thunderstorms; Bob had spent many a stormy night without shelter in the various alleyways of Adelaide, and it took a lot to daunt him these days – in fact he probably would have drifted back off to sleep, if sleep had not quickly become impossible – for now the rain started.

As the thunder and lightning moved slowly across the sky and out to the east, it became very dark. Big drops of rain began to fall. Bob could hear each one as it hit the iron roof.

The drops became louder, and closer together, until soon they were just one long crashing blast from above. The noise was absolutely deafening.

The wind howled and whistled and shook the entire house. Mary's good blue china rattled in the dresser, and Bob decided that now might be a good time to move under the kitchen table.

Sheets of rain lashed the windows, and a few drips from the ceiling saw Mary hurrying about with saucepans to catch the leaks before they stained the floor. Luckily, the cottage was very well built and able to withstand the storm without too much trouble.

It wasn't long before the water was gushing down the outside walls from overflowing gutters and pooling on the hard, dry earth. Water tanks and dams throughout the district – some of which had never even been half full – now overflowed with the heaven-sent water.

Children ran outside to play in the downpour, squealing and splashing in the puddles. Their mothers didn't mind too much – it was such a relief for everyone to have a cool change, and more water than they'd ever hoped for.

Out in the fields, relief for the animals was immediate. The cascading water ran down over their poor, parched bodies, as they lifted their heads up to the sky and literally drank the rain as it fell.

Even though night had now fallen, birds could be heard calling through the pitch darkness – magpies, corellas and galahs – all excited and wide awake, enjoying this longed-for event.

Water was everywhere! It rained without stopping for nearly four days – an almost unheard of event in mid-summer.

Creeks appeared, flowing from the hills in all directions

and running down to form lagoons, which soon became vast lakes; the water from Hutton's lagoon flowed over part of the Broken Hill railway line, and brought with it fences, trees, and any other debris in its path.

Birds never before seen in these parts – such as pelicans, swans, and various herons – miraculously appeared overnight and could be seen swimming, fishing and nesting around the newly formed lakes.

It wasn't long before extravagant boating picnics were being held on most Sundays down at Hutton's lagoon – and William, Mary and Bob were regular attendees of these gatherings. Boats and rafts of all descriptions appeared on the water – some were large and brightly coloured, with exotic names painted on their sides, and others were hurriedly knocked together, homemade affairs – built quickly to take advantage of this wonderous opportunity. Boating parties in the middle of summer were, after all, rather a novelty.

Bob's excited barking carried far across the water, often being long and loud enough to scare the huge gathered flocks of birds into hurried, flapping exits up off the lake and into the sky. Filling the air with their indignant squawking, they soared up and circled around, before coming back down to land again on the rippled blue surface, all the while staring nervously at the dog balanced precariously at the front of the small yellow boat, borrowed for the day from Will's friend, Vic Hutton.

Easter that year was particularly memorable, as railway men and their families from Terowie, Peterborough and Lancelot, all converged at the lagoon for a huge picnic and boat race – pitting themselves against each other for the honour of their respective towns.

Bright, warming sunshine; a perfectly blue, cloudless sky; gaily coloured picnic blankets spread out under the trees; shouts and laughter ringing across the water. The scene was set for a magnificent day.

Bob enjoyed all social gatherings, and the Easter Regatta was to be no exception. William and Mary had been looking forward to it for weeks, and Mary had spent the last two days in a baking frenzy, her cinnamon cake, scones, and sausage rolls all neatly packed in the huge wicker basket William carried carefully under his arm.

All around were happy, smiling faces, warm handshakes and welcoming embraces as friends and colleagues joined the festive group. Everyone was dressed in their best clothes.

By mid-morning there were over two hundred people assembled for the occasion, and a wonderful day was had by all – perhaps with the exception of poor Bob!

The brave little chap had jumped eagerly into the boat with William as he set out for the final race of the day against the lads from Lancelot. These rambunctious fellows, in a much bigger boat than the rest, thought it would be a bit of fun to bump the other, smaller crafts, in a bid to outrun them to the finish line.

William saw with some trepidation that he had been singled out for the next bumping, and braced himself for the impact – but poor old Bob was standing up at the front, and before William had a chance to grab for his collar – WHUMP!

The boat rocked violently, and Bob sailed through the air, landing with a terrific splash and disappearing under the cold blue water. There was a horrified gasp from the onlookers as William started frantically pulling his boots off in order to dive over the side.

Suddenly, there he was, front paws thrashing at the water, eyes tightly closed, bobbing about in a most unhappy way. William quickly leaned out and scooped the bedraggled, soggy dog up into the boat. A great cheer broke out from the banks of the lake, followed by hoots of laughter and applause as Bob stood up and gave a mighty shake, leaving poor William just about as wet as he was!

Bob was never much interested in water sports after the Easter Regatta, and who could blame him? No, he was a dog of the land and, as such, would be sticking strictly to travel by rail from here on in.

CHAPTER SIX
MARCH 1889

Bob wasn't at home much these days.

Most mornings would find him sitting on the platform at Peterborough Station, waiting for his next ride out of town. He didn't mind where he went, it was how he got there that mattered – the trains were now all consuming to him – those great puffing, roaring machines. The excitement! The adventure!

William and Mary had worried at first. Bob would leave the house early and arrive home late, and some nights not at all. The first time he didn't come home, they had barely slept a wink wondering where he was, but the jaunty little dog had breezed in the next evening as if he'd never been away and, eyes bright under the straggly fringe, he'd gone straight over to his spot by the stove to wait for dinner.

'Well!' said Mary, hands on her hips, 'There you are at last! Worried us all sick, you 'ave!'

Bob showed her his most winning smile – those crooked teeth really were strangely appealing! She shook her head wryly and patted the scruffy brown head – he was such a dear little dog, it was impossible to stay cross with him for long. 'Go on then – eat your dinner and we'll say no more about it.'

Needless to say, when Bob failed to return home the next week, William and Mary knew not to worry – they'd heard from Claude Jenkins down in Tarlee that Bob had spent a cosy night on the bed with his two boys, before heading back to the station at dawn to wait for his next ride.

Bob's love of the trains grew stronger every day. He thought of little else but the next journey. The jerky rhythm of the clackety train, the far-reaching views from his eyrie behind the engine, the fascinating smells of coal and steam and his growing kinship with the men all set a fierce stirring in Bob's heart, and had set in motion the beginnings of a legend.

As his confidence grew, Bob's travels took him further afield. It wasn't long before he'd been a visitor to every corner of South Australia that the train tracks would take him to, and he was now regularly venturing out across the border on long haul trips to Sydney. Once or twice he had even crossed the endless Nullabor Plain to travel as far as Perth. Bob had no fear – his trust in the 'loco' crews was unwavering, and he had by now become a very familiar little figure to the railway men of the district.

One advantage of this notoriety was that he never went hungry. Bob enjoyed a wide range of shared lunches with the guards and drivers, and was considered an honoured guest by many of the men. The railway men all knew him and kept an eye out for him, and they'd go home at night and tell stories of the little traveller to their wives and children. The wives re-told these stories in town on their shopping trips, and the children entertained their school friends with the amazing tales of 'Railway Bob.' As these fascinating accounts of his exploits did the rounds of the mid-north, people started to look out for him. Townsfolk living near to the railway lines, particularly in Terowie and Peterborough, always knew when Bob was coming in or out of town – the cheery salutations from his position high atop the coal tender would carry for miles!

Hearing stories of the far-roaming dog from his workmates, William was getting the feeling that the home-loving companion he had envisioned to keep Mary company was probably not Bob. They both loved him dearly (who could resist a dog of such charm and character?) but it was becoming apparent that they would have to share Bob's affections with the wider railway community.

Bob himself had never been happier. The whole world had opened up before him, and every day was a thrilling adventure. His favourite place to be was riding high on a Yankee engine; the big whistle and belching smokestack held an irresistible attraction for him, and his excited barking as the train hauled it's way through towns and hamlets became a familiar part of people's lives.

'There goes Bob! Good ol' Bob!' People would be smiling without even realising.

From the top of the engine, Bob could see for miles, and from this position he had witnessed many amazing scenes.

He was very interested in those great, strange birds, the emus. Always nervous and ready to run at the first sign of danger, their deep 'Booom Booom Boooming' carried far across the plains. From his high vantage point he'd see their long legs pumping in the distance, as they fled in horror. With feathery skirts flying, they ran and zigzagged over the saltbush, for the huge flightless birds were greatly alarmed by the spectre of the train, and desperate to escape its terrifying thunder. Interestingly, they were curious too, often slowing down at a safe distance to look back at the train as it passed by – poised and ready for escape if need be, but drawn to watch just the same.

On one occasion, Bob's fascination with the emus had almost been the end of him. He'd become so excited at the sight of the startled birds in their mad headlong dash across the plain, that he had actually fallen from the train.

Half way between Manoora and Saddleworth, his excited jumping and barking on top of the coal pile had become so fever-pitched that on the final leap, he'd thrown in a bit of a twist and lost his footing. The next thing he knew, he was flying through the air with legs and tail flailing, and then hitting the ground with an almighty thump – all the wind knocked out of him.

As he lay gasping on the prickly grass, Bob could see the blinking light on the back of the guards van growing smaller and fainter as the train continued on its journey, unaware of the drama it had left behind.

Poor Bob watched the train until it finally disappeared over the horizon, and the silence and the huge blue sky above him were all that was left.

After lying perfectly still for what seemed many hours, but was probably really just a few minutes, Bob's breathing started to feel a little easier, the world around him stopped spinning, and he began to feel that perhaps he could try to get up.

Clambering unsteadily to his feet, he yelped in pain as a horrible spasm shot up one of his back legs, and he stood still for a while, sides heaving, and shaking all over in distress and shock.

What a terrible thing to happen – and all so suddenly. He'd been having such an enjoyable day, and now look! Stranded in the middle of nowhere, with no hope of rescue, things were suddenly looking pretty grim.

There was nothing for it but to walk back to Manoora. The town was miles away, and Bob knew it would take him a long time, but the indomitable spirit which had kept him going through all his previous tribulations was now coming to the fore again.

Hour after hour, slow step after slow step, the poor little dog limped carefully through the afternoon on his three good legs, following the railway tracks back the way he had come. Luckily the weather had been very mild, and he even found a puddle or two for a drink along the way.

It was a heart wrenching and quite pitiful sight that greeted Horace Tingwell as he staggered out of the goods shed at the back of the Manoora Railway Station. Weighed down with an armload of heavy tools, he was about to start loading up the cart for an early start the next morning, when movement in the distance caught his eye. Squinting into the late afternoon sun, it took Horace a moment or two to be certain of what he was seeing.

A limping brown dog with blood encrusted around his face was lurching up the middle of the tracks – head down, ears flat, tail tucked between his legs and covered all over in prickles, he was the very picture of misery

Horace stared blankly at this apparition for a few seconds until recognition suddenly dawned on him.

'Gawd all bloody mighty,' he yelled, 'It's Bob!' Horror-struck, he dropped his tools and ran up the track to meet the poor little bundle, scooping the dog safely up into his big tree-trunk arms.

'There's the poor liddle lad,' he said in the most soothing tone he could muster, 'What the bloody 'ell 'ave you been up to, fella?'

He carried Bob into the shed and laid him gently onto a pile of blankets,

'Don' worry matey, you'll be orright now!'

Bob was a particular friend of Horace's, and the huge burly workman was just about reduced to tears when he saw the terrible state of the usually cheery and bright eyed little dog. Carefully looking him over, it didn't take Horace long to figure out what had happened.

'Didja fall off the train, ol' lad? Lord, it's a bloody wonder you weren't killed!' (Horace was well known for his love of the word 'Bloody,' which he used with relish at every possible opportunity.)

By now, a small crowd of men had gathered in the shed. They all stood around the makeshift bed of old blankets and waited worriedly for Horace's diagnosis. Looking up at the concerned faces of his friends, Bob's tail beat weakly up and down in pleasure to see them.

Horace had finished his gentle probing of Bob's injuries and pronounced his opinion to the crew.

'That leg's not broke, but 'e's given it a fair ol' wrench, 'e's bitten 'is tongue, an' the rest of 'im's black an' blue. I'd say 'e's bin pretty bloody lucky all round, 'cos it could 'ave bin a lot bloody worse!'

Everyone was very relieved, and Horace volunteered to care for Bob until he was fully recovered. Once this had been agreed upon, the fire was stoked and the billy put on to boil as dinner pails were opened and the evening shift began.

Bob lay motionless on the blankets. His poor little body ached all over and horrible pains shot up and down his leg whenever he tried to move. He could hear himself panting, and every now and then someone would appear at his side and gently lift his head to offer him a drink. Comforted by the close proximity of the men, and feeling warm and safe on his pile of blankets, the hushed voices and occasional quiet laughter of Horace and the others eventually lulled him off to sleep.

The next morning found Bob feeling a little better. His body ached and he was stiff all over, but the pain in his leg had miraculously faded to a dull throb, and he was able to get himself up and walk about slowly on the shed floor, albeit a bit unsteadily at first. Horace was very pleased with his progress, and served him up a steaming bowl of porridge for breakfast, much to Bob's disgust.

'There yer go laddie, that'll soon 'ave yer feelin' better – I allus say t'aint nothin' nicer'n a big serve o' porridge in the mornin' ter set yer on yer way!'

Bob sniffed tentatively at the bowl, but the smell of the oats and milk was decidedly unappealing. He stared hopefully up at Horace.

'Now don' look at me like that, it's mighty good for yer an' none of the other lads complain.' There was much eye rolling and hands around throats in the background – which luckily went unnoticed by Horace, whose heart of gold was firmly in place, and completely incorruptible.

★

A few days later and Bob was just about back to his old self. He'd left the goods shed at Manoora and had travelled back to Peterborough with Horace on Tuesday afternoon.

Word of Bob's accident had spread quickly throughout the district, and a relieved Mary – and most of the Peterborough crew – were waiting at the station to meet him. As the train pulled in, Bob (riding safely inside the carriage this time) was whimpering and scrabbling at the door in his hurry to be out. He had missed William and Mary, and his box by the stove, and he was very, very glad to be home.

★

Although his accident did not seem to affect Bob's love of riding the coal tender (he was back up on top of the train within a week), Bob walked with a slight limp for quite a few months afterwards, and even though the excited barking and yodelling was just as loud and enthusiastic as ever – a fact attested to by townsfolk and railway staff from far and wide – he was never again seen jumping up and down on top of the train!

CHAPTER SEVEN
JUNE 1889

Will read the letter again, not quite believing what he'd read the first time.

'On and after Monday 6th June 1889, your Home Station will, until further notice, be Perth Central Station, Western Australia.'

'Bloody Hell! Transfer papers! To Western Australia!' This was a most unexpected turn of events.

Will knew that a nomadic life was often the lot of the railway man, and he'd been transferred a few times over the course of his career, but this one was a bit of a shock.

Peterborough had come to feel like home over the past few years – he'd grown very fond of the busy little town, and there were many good friends here he would be sorry to leave – and Gawd almighty, how on earth was he going to tell Mary?

★

The first pink flush of dawn was edging over the horizon as William finished his breakfast, pulled on his jacket and prepared to leave for work.

The kitchen was brightly lit, and as he kissed Mary goodbye he could see the tears glistening in her eyes. She hadn't said much since he'd showed her the transfer papers last night, but a tightly gripped handkerchief and quiet, intermittent sniffing told him the rest of the story.

William hugged his much loved wife tightly against his chest, her hair soft against his cheek. 'Listen Love, I know it's a bit of a shock, but we've got a few weeks to get used to the idea, and who knows, once we get to Perth we might even find that we enjoy city living – we can go to a show on Saturday nights, and just think how you'll love the shopping!'

Mary gulped back her tears. William's empathy made her feel like crying even more, and she didn't want him to feel any worse – after all, there really wasn't much they could do about it now; they'd just have to try and make the best of things.

★

The day of William and Mary's departure came. They both felt pretty gloomy, and didn't have much to say to each other as they stood out in the street, bags at their feet, taking one last look at their cheerful little cottage before heading over to the station to begin the long journey across the country to Western Australia. By this stage, Mary's eyes were very red, and she was sniffing a lot into her hankie. William put his arm around her and squeezed a bit for comfort, but there really wasn't anything to say.

Bright, warming sunshine, the kind that feels good on your back on a cool morning, spread golden rays across the wide plains. Powdery white clouds streaked across the sky, and somewhere in the near distance, a rowdy group of apostle birds could be heard karkling and squarkling over some tasty food item.

William and Mary climbed onto the train with heavy hearts, looking out of the window for the last time at the town that had been their home for four happy years.

Mary was feeling quite desolate. Starting all over again was always hard – setting up house, getting a veggie garden started, making new friends – it was all so daunting, and just the thought of it set her off into fresh floods of hot tears.

Suddenly William was shaking her arm.

'Mary, look Love, it's Bob – come to say goodbye!'

Peering through the window, wiping her eyes with her best hankie, she could see her beloved little dog sitting on the platform, Horace's hand on his collar. They hadn't seen Bob for a while, and had struggled for many days with the decision they'd both eventually agreed on – to leave him behind. It hadn't been easy – the thought of never seeing the dear little chap again was very hard to take, but his obvious affinity with the trains and the railway men, and especially his determined independence and free spirit, had made them realise that he really wasn't their dog anymore. Moreover, Bob was not a dog who would ever be happy living in a suburban backyard – they both knew that, and they wanted only the best for him. Horace had faithfully promised Mary to keep an eye on him wherever possible, and that was as much as they could do.

So the train pulled slowly out of the station, taking William and Mary far away to the other side of the country and leaving Bob in the care of his new family – the railway men.

CHAPTER EIGHT
DECEMBER 31 1891

It was Sunday, and not far past dawn.

A soft tinge of pink still hovered in the pale morning sky, and the incessant clamourings of a baby magpie as it followed its parents around the front yard begging for food, could be heard clearly from the bedroom.

George Hiscock, lying comfortably in bed on his only day off, was wide awake, having had his dozing interrupted by one of his rare, but brilliant ideas. The only thing was, he was going to need the co-operation of his friend Bob the Railway Dog.

★

Bob had arrived back in Terowie late the previous night after spending a few days over in Port Augusta. The ever cheerful little traveller had trotted confidently home with George at the end of his shift, where he had been warmly received by George's wife and their young daughter Rosie. After dinner (a delicious meal of warm mutton casserole, eaten under the table), Bob had spent a cosy night tucked up on the end of

Rosie's bed, listening with interest as she read to him from her favourite storybook, and licking her little hand with affection as she eventually drifted off to sleep.

As morning dawned, George had awakened with the sudden realisation that here before him was a perfect opportunity to get the 'Drivers Dog' into his studio for a sitting. Suddenly gripped with excitement and resolve, he clambered out of bed and dressed quickly, fumbling with buttons and laces in his haste to be underway with his plans.

Now, at this point it should be said that George Hiscock, a veteran locomotive fireman of twenty years, and dedicated follower of the local Terowie cricket team, was also a very keen and talented amateur photographer.

He had set up a little space for his hobby in the lean-to behind the kitchen, and had purchased the latest Box Brownie camera from a salesman he knew down in Adelaide. Various friends and relations had sat for him, with most going away very pleased with the results. Although he had dabbled occasionally with various photographic styles and subjects, George felt most confident with his studio portraits – and today he intended to take that idea one step further and immortalise 'Bob the Railway Dog' on film for all to see.

Bob was an obliging fellow and allowed himself to be lifted up and carefully positioned on top of a large wooden crate, over which George had draped his wife's much revered patterned bedspread. The getting of this irreplaceable family heirloom for his photograph had involved careful planning and subterfuge (ever so quietly removing the quilt from the bed and tip-toeing down the hall and out through the back door to his studio).

When Mrs Hiscock noticed this sacrilege later, George

received a long and loud telling off, but, as he told the fellows down at the pub that evening, it was worth all the yelling because he'd already got the picture he wanted and no-one could take that away from him now!

★

As George viewed the scene through his lens, he could see it still didn't look quite right – it needed just that little something extra. As he scanned around the room for ideas, inspiration suddenly dawned.

He hurried out to the shed, returning several minutes later – dusty and out of breath, but triumphant – with two old lanterns and an oil can. 'The perfect props for a railway dog!' he thought happily.

Bob was still sitting obediently on the box, and stood up expectantly with his tail wagging as George re-entered the room.

'Good boy, Bob!' said George, patting the soft mop head 'Good, good dog!'

Bob grinned and held his paw up for a shake.

George wrote his name and the date on a piece of card, and pinned it to the quilt before arranging his ornaments carefully around the cheerful brown dog. He then bent down to view the scene through his lens. 'Perfect! Absolutely – Bloody well – perfect!'

Bob stared straight into the camera and flashed his most winning smile.

CLICK.

One shot was all he needed, and George knew exactly what he would do with the picture. His plans were made, his anticipation high.

Later that afternoon, barricaded in his tiny darkroom, George placed the special photographic paper carefully into a tray of developing fluid, and watched with relief and pride as Bob's friendly eyes and engaging smile appeared like magic on the paper.

What a beautiful photograph!

If only George could have known at that moment how eternal this wonderful image would be…

★

It was three weeks later, and word had got around pretty quickly that George was handing out gift cards depicting the enigmatic 'Driver's Dog' in all his glory. Everywhere he went, George found himself inundated with requests for the cards. He happily printed out many copies for the lads down at the yards, and also for his neighbours, friends, relatives, and anyone else who asked.

This endearing image of the jaunty, smiling dog found its way into many homes, wallets and back pockets, and George found himself enjoying the trappings of fame for a while – which mostly entailed having beers bought for him at the pub, and friendly nods and smiles from all who passed him on the street.

The whole undertaking had proved such a success that the following year he created a new portrait of 'The Railway Dog' – much to the delight of Bob's many friends and admirers.

These lovely photographs were treasured keepsakes to the railway workers who knew Bob, and were kept by many as family heirlooms to be handed down to their children and grandchildren. The much-talked-about little dog gazed down from pride of place on many a mantelpiece around the country — he was, after all, a heartfelt reminder of 'the good old days' and would be long and lovingly remembered by all who knew him.

CHAPTER NINE
OCTOBER 1892

There was a man standing under the trees up ahead. Even from this distance, Bob could tell there was something not quite right about him, and unfortunately his instinct was about to be proved correct.

Bob was trotting with brisk purpose up the winding dirt road that led out to the showgrounds. The sheep sales were on today, and Bob already knew (having attended this event last year) that at the final fall of the hammer, the CWA* ladies would appear like magic with their trestle tables and starched white cloths, ready to serve tea and cakes and biscuits while the men put on an enormous and seemingly never-ending barbeque.

There was no way Bob was going to risk missing any part of this great event, so he was intending to arrive early, and maybe enjoy a bit of a dust-up with one or two of the local sheepdogs while he waited for the food to appear.

A bend in the track had until now hidden the man from view, although Bob knew he was there, having already caught a whiff of his rather unpleasant odour. As the man came into sight up ahead, Bob decided he didn't like the look of him much – his clothes were torn and dirty, and a long grey beard covered most of his face. He was leaning casually against a battered four-wheeled wagon, a vehicle which had surely seen better days – as had the sway-backed brown mare hitched (much too tightly) to the front of it. Although the horse gave a snort when Bob appeared around the corner, the man, busy smoking an evil smelling pipe and staring intently up at the sky, gave no sign of having noticed him at all.

There was no-one else in sight.

Feeling a bit uneasy as he approached the man, Bob gave him a wide berth as their paths crossed.

Having been treated with nothing but kindness and respect by the people of the mid-north, Bob was given a terrible fright when a hard, strong hand suddenly descended upon his scruff and lifted him up into the air. He yelped and struggled, but was powerless to escape as he was dropped neatly into a hessian bag and thrown onto the back of the wagon.

The next couple of hours were the most frightening of Bob's life; the jerking and rocking wagon bounced him around on top of the various hard and pointed objects sharing his confinement. If possible, the worst was yet to come; when the wagon finally came to a halt, the man climbed down and just walked away, leaving Bob still tied up in the stinking bag, terrified and alone as night fell and it began to rain.

After what seemed like an eternity of fear and hunger and discomfort, Bob heard the man returning. Before he had time to try and get a bite at him through the hessian, he was yanked up and out, and the foul smelling bag was finally untied.

Blinking and shaking his head, he found himself in a dark shed with no windows, but enough cracks in the walls to let in a bit of light and an icy cold, swirling wind. Bob snarled and bared his teeth at the horrible man, and got a smack over the nose in reply. The rough, cruel hands tied a heavy piece of rope around his neck, and secured the other end tightly to a metal ring in the wall. As the door slammed behind him, and Bob was left alone in the dark, the awful truth finally dawned on him – he was a prisoner, with no hope of escape.

Bob spent the rest of the night barking and howling and pulling on the rope, but all to no avail. He was hungry and thirsty. He realised eventually that no-one was going to come for him – not Horace, or Will or John or Harold – he was alone, and at the mercy of the tatty, bearded man.

Without doubt, this was even worse than being caught by the Council Dog Catcher all those years ago – at least then he'd been treated kindly and given a decent meal. No, this time things were looking exceedingly bleak, and Bob was scared – very scared. As the first grey light of dawn seeped through the gaps in the rough wooden walls of his prison, Bob was able to see a bit more of his surroundings.

Hanging from rusty hooks high above were hundreds and hundreds of rabbit skins. He knew what rabbits were – after all, they'd almost been his destiny. It seemed like forever ago that Will had rescued him from an uncertain fate hunting with the rabbiting gangs up in Carrieton. Funnily enough, Bob had never been much interested in rabbits, although he'd watched a wedge-tailed eagle swoop down and carry one away once.

From his perch high atop the coal tender, clickety-clacking

along somewhere between Hallett and Mt Bryan, Bob had watched the drama unfold in the distance – the great wings of the eagle outstretched, the talons reaching down, and the poor rabbit being scooped up and carried away before he'd even realised the danger that was upon him.

The sight and smell of such death all around him filled Bob with fresh fear, and the poor dog pressed himself up tightly against the wall, shaking and whimpering. It was as pathetic and heart-rending a sight as you would ever see.

In the meantime, quiet footsteps were approaching the shed. They came to a halt right outside the door, and for a moment there was silence. Bob's ears pricked up. Slowly and quietly the door opened – just a crack. Bob, his hackles standing on end and his teeth bared ferociously, was ready to fight! Snarling and growling like a wild animal, he would have been unrecognizable to his friends from home as the sweet natured, cheery little dog they all knew and loved.

A face appeared in the crack but whoever it was, having taken one look at the apparently vicious, snarling dog, straining on the end of a long piece of frayed rope, shut the door again rather quickly! Bob stopped barking and listened, his ears pricked and his head tilted to one side. Whispered voices could be heard outside – childish voices. 'Sssh! Dad'll be really mad if 'e catches us!' There was silence for a few moments before the door opened again, and this time three faces appeared in the gap, two down low, and one up higher – all looking a bit wary, and ready to slam the door shut in an instant if need be. He growled menacingly, and, sure enough the door was quickly closed again.

'Don't do it Bertie – 'e'll kill us all – an' then maybe eat us too!'

Bob was a bit bewildered by this turn of events. Quiet now, he stared at the door with big eyes as it opened for a third time, revealing three curious children. Giggling and squealing, the two smaller ones took turns trying to push each other through the doorway, thrilled by their fear and daring – not yet aware that in Bob, they met absolutely no danger whatsoever.

Bob stood up, puffing, his tail wagging tentatively.

'Look Floss! 'e's not savage – 'e's waggin 'is tail at us – I bet I could pat 'im too!' and without further ado, a small boy stepped over the threshold with hand outstretched.

'Bertie no!' called a frightened voice. A tall, sweet faced girl, older than the others, jumped forward through the doorway and grabbed the boy's arm.

'No look Sis – 'e's just 'ungry – poor liddle chap! Try a bit o' this fella.' The little boy held out a rather nasty looking morsel which Bob sniffed for a moment, and then grabbed off his hand, eating wolfishly while staring guiltily at the boy – he was so hungry he had forgotten his manners! As if to make amends for his impropriety, Bob sat down politely and held his paw up for a shake. The children, their fear forgotten, pushed their way into the shed and stood in front of the dog, each one taking their turn to solemnly shake the little paw as they looked him over.

'Wonder where Dad found 'im? 'e don't look like a stray,' said Floss, the youngest of the three.

'No,' said Bertie thoughtfully ''e don't look like no stray, Floss, cos I'd bet you anythink you like 'e isn't! I reckon Dad's pinched 'im from somewhere – 'an don't look at me like that Kate, 'cos you know I'm right!'

Kate was going to be a rare beauty, but didn't know it

yet. She was fourteen, and so far had spent her teenage years doing her best to look after the young ones – Bertie, who was eleven and didn't take kindly to his sister bossing him about, and Floss, the baby, who would be six this year; not that their father would remember. Dad had turned to the drink when their much loved mother had died of consumption – although Kate, ever full of romantic notions, was quite sure that her poor, frail mother had died of a broken heart, having had all her hopes and dreams battered out of her by a shiftless husband and years of disappointments. When Mum had first become ill, Grandma Buckle had appeared on their doorstep one morning with bulging suitcases and a cheery smile, ready to nurse her ailing daughter and look after the children.

She'd never left.

Kate often lifted her eyes up to the sky and thanked God for their deliverance. As awful as it had been losing their mother, Kate could only imagine with dread what their lives would have been like without their straightforward, no nonsense, wonderful grandmother to care for them all.

Grandma Buckle was determined that Kate's life, and those of her brother and sister would not disappear into oblivion the same way their mother's had, and she worked hard to show the children they were much loved, while also making sure they attended school regularly so one day there'd be a chance for them all to leave this place and get a proper start in life. It was her dream for all of them, and she was determined to make it happen.

Their father didn't figure much in her plans, for as far as she could tell, he'd never really cared for them much and, apart from the odd grunt thrown in their direction, he never spoke to them at all. In fact, most of the time he was up in the hills trapping rabbits, so they didn't see much of him anyway. He could be gone for days, even weeks at a time, but always left money on the kitchen table for her to buy food and supplies with. That was one good thing, she supposed – he hadn't let them actually starve yet, although she did yearn for a little extra to buy the girls at least one pretty dress each, and maybe a pair of pink satin slippers for Kate.

'Aah one day,' she told herself, 'when our ship comes in.'

Out in the shed, the children knew that both Dad and Grandma were going to be very angry with them if they were caught with the dog – albeit for quite different reasons. Kate filled a bucket with water from the pump behind the wash house. She carried it in for the dog and the poor little thing just drank and drank. Bertie and Floss appeared, having raided the kitchen pantry while Grandma was hanging out the washing. Feeling quite excited about their secret, they resolved to care for their new pet whilst pretending complete ignorance to their father. The children knew that he would take the dog with him when he went rabbiting up in the hills, but that didn't mean they couldn't have him for their very own pet while Dad was at home – they'd just have to be a bit sneaky, that's all! Bertie still said, and the girls agreed, that the dog was obviously someone's pet, and that Dad had no doubt stolen him to go hunting with. As it turned out, they were right.

At dawn the next morning, the horrible man opened the shed door with a bang and untied the end of the rope that held Bob prisoner. Pulling away in fear, Bob found himself being hauled over to the wagon and retied tightly to the back of it. As the skinny old horse clopped wearily out of the yard, Bob quickly realised he had two choices: jog along behind, or be dragged by the neck. He jogged.

After what seemed like endless miles, the wagon finally pulled to a halt beneath a small grove of trees, and the man placed a tin bowl of water on the ground in front of Bob. This small act of kindness was a surprise, but Bob wasn't going to be won over that easily.

For the next few days, Bob was dragged about on the end of a piece of rope while the man tried to entice him into chasing rabbits and digging up burrows. Bob was having none of it. To the man's credit, he never hit Bob again, but he certainly did a lot of swearing and jumping up and down. The dog just stared blankly up at him as he cursed and swore. The man had been pretty confident that Bob would turn out to be a real beaut little rabbiter – and crikey, had he been wrong about that! The bloody dog didn't have a clue.

If the man had known that Bob was way too smart to be forced into killing rabbits when he really didn't want to, things may have been different but, as it turned out, he'd found the dog to be pretty good company on his hunting trips, so the man decided to keep him, even though the useless mutt was too stupid to hunt!

So this routine went on for about four months – the father took Bob out with him on all his hunting trips, and no longer bothered to hide the dog's presence at home, allowing the children, after much begging and pleading, to care for Bob and have him for their very own pet. He was even allowed into the house.

'Will wonders ever cease?' thought Grandma Buckle. Since the arrival of the dog, she'd noticed the relationship between the man and his children changing, and much for the better. He actually spoke to them these days, and every now and then they'd even get a smile out of him. This was unheard of! Grandma Buckle didn't say anything, but she knew it was all down to the dog – a ratty, unkempt little thing with awful teeth, but Lord, he had beautiful manners. She couldn't help but like him, even though she'd never been much of a dog person. Anyway, whatever it was, life was much more pleasant these days, and she certainly wasn't going to rock the boat. The man never spoke of where the dog had come from, and none of them dared to ask, mostly because they had a pretty good idea anyway.

So the man was really asking for trouble when he decided unexpectedly to take Bob, the children and Grandma Buckle into town to sell off his latest wagonload of rabbit skins. The skins were fetching a very reasonable price at the time, and perhaps the man's optimism overshadowed his good sense – for within three minutes of the overloaded wagon pulling up behind the Jamestown railway station, Bob had been recognised.

As fate would have it, Horace Tingwell had chosen that particular moment to walk down the steps at the back of the station. His eyes nearly popped out of his head when he saw Bob – the look on his face was quite comical as he suddenly realised who he was looking at!

'Why, it's Bob! Bob! You bloody liddle beaut! I can't bloody believe it – we all thought you wuz dead young fella! Hey lads – get out 'ere!' he shouted loudly over his shoulder, 'You'll never bloody guess what's 'appened – come out and see who's turned up!' Three men, all chewing and holding battered tin mugs, (they were halfway through their lunch) appeared in the doorway. All three faces lit up as they recognised their long–lost friend. For the next few minutes, there was much excited barking and patting and exclaiming at the wonder of it all – but inevitably, their attention soon turned to the man, the old lady and the three children sitting open-mouthed on the back of the shabby wagon piled high with skins.

'Dad's really gonna cop it now!' whispered Bertie excitedly. 'I knew he'd get caught for stealin' the dog – now you watch – we'll all be goin' to jail!'

Floss started to cry.

'Sssh Bertie!' hissed Grandma Buckle, 'No-one's going to jail.' But privately, she wasn't so sure – these big railway men were looking pretty irate, and they were obviously waiting for an explanation.

'I've bin a bloody fool,' lamented the rabbit hunter, climbing wearily down to face the angry men. He knew he was in real trouble this time and, as he looked apprehensively at the circle of angry faces and clenched fists, he realised that it was time to try to tell the truth.

Bob's happy influence on his household had changed the man more than he realised, and as he confessed all to the men, he was surprised to see their expressions change from anger to understanding. He thought he even saw a little compassion. Luckily for the rabbit hunter, the railway men were a decent and honest group of men and although they remained livid about the way poor Bob had been stolen from them, they could also understand how the whole family had fallen in love with him, and laughed uproariously when they heard about the man's vain attempts to teach Bob how to hunt rabbits!

It was sad, very sad, Horace thought later to himself – the

man had no social skills at all, and lived on a meagre selection out in the hills, trying to make a living out of his rabbit traps. That poor family. Those little kiddies! Horace shook his head and resolved to tell his wife the whole story tonight at tea – she and her CWA ladies would sort something out for them, he was sure, but in the meantime, he knew Reg O' Brian's kelpie bitch had three beaut little puppies looking for homes, and he intended to take one out for that skinny little lad the first chance he got.

So the bush telegraph was set in motion, and over the next few weeks, great changes were made in the lives of the rabbit trapper's family. He had vowed to himself that he would make a fresh start in life, and he began straight away. From that day forward, his family came first. They now had friends, the children had new clothes, Kate was taking music lessons, and Grandma Buckle had joined the CWA.

And last but not least, Bertie had a beautiful new puppy, named 'Bob' after the dog who changed their lives, and who none of them would ever forget.

*Country Womens Association

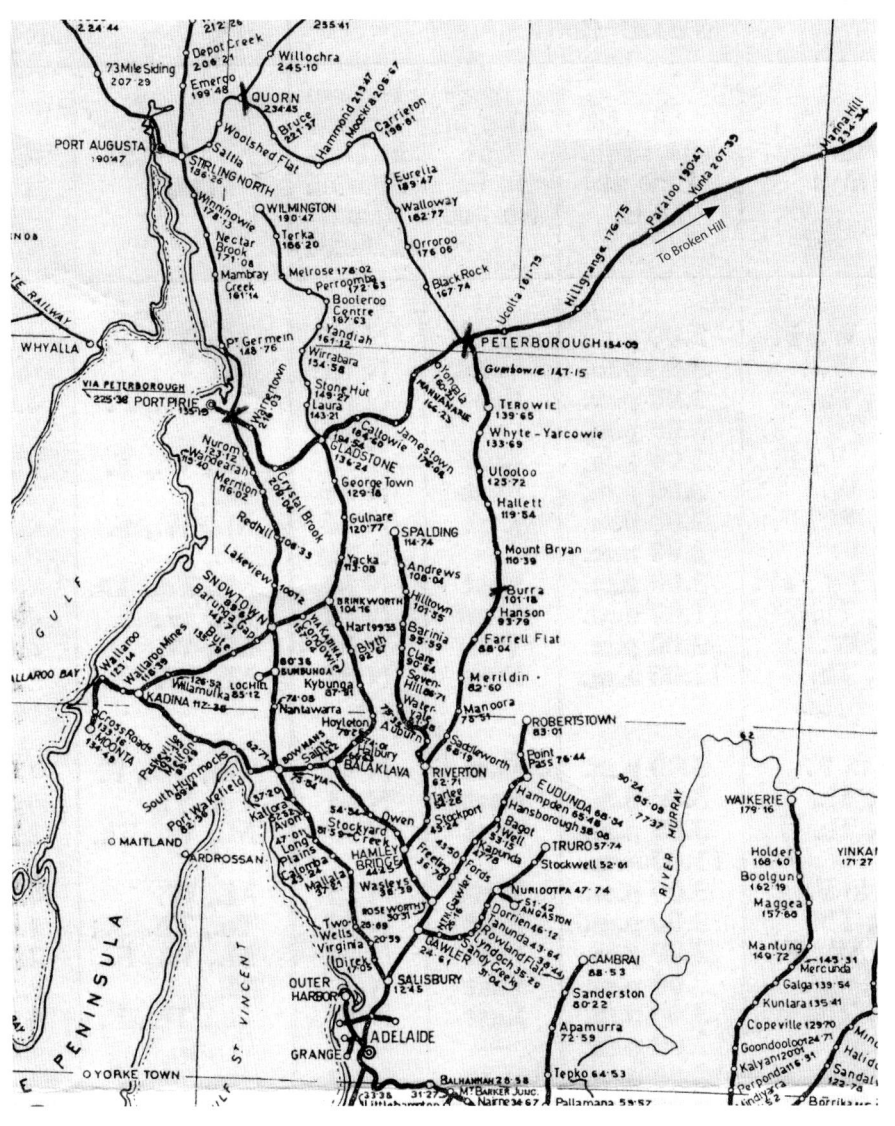

Above: Railway map of relevant areas

Above: Terowie Railway Station
Below: Bob the Railway Dog at Port Augusta c. 1887
Photographs courtesy of State Library of South Australia

Above: Bob the Railway Dog 1892
Photograph courtesy of State Library of South Australia

Above: Burra Railway Station
Below: Peterborough Hotel

"BOB" THE RAILWAY DOG'S COLLAR

Above: 'Bob's collar' photograph courtesy of Reg Pye
Below: 'Bob sat on the grassy verge at the top of Government Road, looking down upon the township of Peterborough spread out below.'

Above: McMurtrie family gravestones at Lancelot cemetery

Above: Bob the Railway Dog 1892
Photograph courtesy of State Library of South Australia

Above: Bob the Railway Dog 1892
Photograph courtesy of State Library of South Australia

CHAPTER TEN
APRIL 1893

Harry Caire was a travelling salesman. On the first of each month, he would load his bulging cases onto the train at Adelaide Station and begin the long journey north as far as Beltana, and then back down to Peterborough and across to Port Pirie.

Stopping in each town along the line, Harry would display his wares from a room booked at the nearest hotel and lately, he was pleased to say, business had been booming.

Harry had a lot going for him. As a seller of ladies fineries, he carried a large array of pretty dress fabrics, lace samples and ribbons, so he was always a very popular visitor with the women of these rural towns. It also hadn't gone unnoticed that he was almost impossibly handsome – tall and lean, with dark hair, grey eyes, and a quirky, lopsided grin which had been setting girls' hearts a-flutter all over the country. There were always queues of excited women around Harry's stalls as, for many of them, the chances to buy nice things for themselves were very few and far between.

Harry really enjoyed his work – he loved the travel, and never grew tired of watching the ever-changing landscape unfold through the carriage windows as he zigzagged his way across the beautiful mid-north. Because of his frequent journeying, he had also made some very good friends amongst the loco crews, and so was never short of company and conversation over a drink in the evenings. But Harry secretly reckoned that the best thing about being a travelling salesman was to see the lit-up faces of his lady customers as they rummaged through the fabrics and laces trying to make a decision. He was such a nice and humble young man... he never quite realised the lit up faces were often as much due to him as his wares.

★

Harry had, over the years, shared many a journey with Bob the Railway Dog. With both of them being in the business of long distance rail travel, they would often find themselves on the same train. Of course, with Harry sitting inside the carriage, and Bob riding up on top of the coal tender, they really only saw each other on the station platforms and outside various tearooms and hotels, but Harry and Bob were firm friends just the same.

One Tuesday evening, about three weeks after his dramatic rescue from the rabbit trapper, Bob was sitting outside the Peterborough Hotel waiting to walk home with George Hiscock. It was very dark beyond the lights from the windows, and a cool breeze ruffled the soft brown fur around his neck. From the shadows, a quiet cough and the flare of a match set Bob growling, until a familiar voice called out of the gloom, 'Bob lad! Is that you? How are ya, fella?'

It was Harry, out for a last quiet smoke before bed, and Bob was, as always, very pleased to see his old friend.

Tail whipping madly from side to side, he licked Harry's outstretched hand most enthusiastically – it had been months since they'd last met.

Harry had heard the story of Bob's abduction and, like everyone else, was greatly relieved when the little dog had been returned home safely to his friends. Even so, the drama still worried him. Kneeling down beside Bob, he fingered the old leather strap around the dog's neck. It actually looked like a piece of horse's rein or something similar, and the dry leather was cracked and brittle – it was rubbing a bare patch in his fur, and was certainly no longer suitable for wearing as a collar.

Harry was brewing one of his 'great ideas' and, while his hands automatically rubbed Bob's chest, his thoughts were elsewhere; he nodded to himself as a plan slowly began to take shape.

First thing the next morning, Harry was down at the rail yards looking for Merv Lillywhite, an old friend of his father's, and a man he was sure would be able to help him with his project.

Merv was a brass worker, and very good at his job. When Harry told him of his plan to commission a collar for Bob the railway dog, Merv said, 'Bloody lovely idea mate! I'll be a part o' that; jus' tell me what yer after an' I'll do me best!'

Much relieved, Harry filled him in on all the details.

★

Large tubs of pink geraniums arranged carefully around the walls of the Peterborough Station building made an attractive and colourful display for passengers disembarking from the midday train.

As Harry stepped down onto the platform, the bright sunlight dazzled him for a moment, so he didn't see the row of excited female faces pressed against the tearoom window as he passed by!

In his suitcase, carefully wrapped in a piece of calico, was a black leather collar which Harry had bought from an exclusive leather goods shop in Adelaide, after much careful deliberation and umming and aaaing. It had cost a bit more than he'd wanted to pay, but it was by far the nicest one he'd seen, and Bob 'The Wonder Dog' was well worth it, he reckoned.

Harry's first stop after dropping his bags off at the Peterborough Hotel, was to the rail yards, where he planned to meet up with Merv. Harry felt quite excited about the brass nameplate he'd commissioned for the collar and could already picture how smart Bob would look wearing it.

As he strode up the track towards the yards, Harry tilted his hat down over his eyes and whistled a little ditty he'd heard over on the docks in Port Pirie. It was lunch time and he could see Merv up in the distance, sitting on a wooden crate out under one of the huge pepper trees that grew alongside the sheds. Leaning back against the rough bark and sipping tea from a battered enamel mug, Merv appeared to have not a care in the world. A cool breeze rustled through the soft, fern-like leaves, and a busy trail of ants went about their business in the dry earth around his feet.

'Hey Merv!' called Harry, as he approached the old man 'How's tricks, mate?'

'Aaah, it's young 'arry come back at last!' said Merv, climbing stiffly to his feet. 'Come on lad, I know what yer 'ere for, an' it's come up a bloody treat if I do say so meself!'

Harry followed the old man into the dim light of the shed and looked on with pleasure and relief as Merv brought out the metal plate for his inspection. It was perfect! Harry handed over the leather collar he'd carried up in his pocket, and then watched with interest as Merv got to work on it with a couple of large flat rivets.

Ten minutes later and the job was done. It was a very impressive collar – black leather with a brass mounted name plate which read, Stop me not but let me jog, for I am Bob the drivers' dog. SAR'*

★

Harry was thrilled! He pumped Merv's hand most enthusiastically, and slapped him on the back a couple of times for good measure. He couldn't wait to track Bob down and try it on for size.

As luck would have it, Harry and Bob's paths crossed just a few days later at the busy and very beautiful Burra Railway Station.

Bob's tail was a blur, wagging in all directions as he wove around Harry's legs and trod on his shoes. Harry was laughing as he tried to extricate himself from the excited dog's welcome. Eventually Bob calmed down enough to sit and hold his paw up for a shake.

Harry rummaged in his bag and pulled out the collar. He was a bit nervous as to whether the dog would take to it or not, having worn nothing but the tatty old rein around his neck all these years. Kneeling down, he showed Bob the collar and let him sniff it thoroughly before he buckled it firmly into place. Bob didn't seem to mind at all – in fact, Harry fancied the little chap almost knew how handsome he looked as he barked and jumped up and down: showing off, Harry thought!

Yes, the collar had turned out to be all that Harry had hoped for, and in the future he knew there'd be no fear of the little dog being mistaken for anyone other than who he was – Bob the Railway Dog.

*South Australian Railways

CHAPTER ELEVEN
FEBRUARY 1894

The midday train to Broken Hill was boarding at Adelaide Station. The daily ritual of hurrying passengers, voices and laughter, hugs and kisses, loading of baggage, and the intermittent whistle blowing and flag waving by bustling, important, uniformed men, was in full swing.

Swirling white clouds of steam huffed and puffed from the mighty engines, blanketing the whole scene with an air of mystery, and possibilities of adventure that Bob found completely irresistible.

Today, he was snaking his way through the crowds on the platform, brown eyes shining, tail waving madly and heart brimming with excitement – he loved a trip to Broken Hill!

His intention was to ride the train all the way up to the busy mining town and to stay the night with John McDonald, the engine driver. It was a long journey, which made it a good journey as far as Bob was concerned. Tomorrow, he might jump aboard one of the long goods trains heading out over the vast plains and mountains to Sydney – he knew the men would look out for him on the lengthy trip, so he never worried about going hungry or finding somewhere to sleep.

Every once in a while, and usually only if the weather was very bad, Bob could be found travelling in the relative comfort of the train's interior.

On this particular day, a great dark storm had been brewing on the horizon since early morning, and it finally rolled in over the city just as the train was pulling out of Adelaide. An icy wind sprang up, howling and whipping around the train, hurling dust and debris against the windows, and rocking the carriages quite violently. It was freezing cold outside, with huge black clouds overhead promising imminent rain, so Bob had decided fairly quickly that a visit with his old friend George Hiscock in the guards van (and possibly even the sharing of this affable man's dinner in front of the little coal heater) was much the preferable option.

★

It was at this moment that Fate quietly stepped in – as she often does – with Bob about to become witness to a small part of a much larger tale – a story so heartbreaking that it was remembered around the district with much regret for many years to come…

★

One of the passengers on the train that afternoon was a man called Thomas McMurtrie. Thomas was a stocky, grey-haired man with ruddy cheeks and clear, far-sighted eyes that spoke of long years spent outdoors through all seasons. He walked with a slight limp (a souvenir from a run-in with the plough a few years back) and spoke in a heavy Scottish brogue which made his grandchildren giggle.

Thomas's wife Bess had died three years earlier, leaving a wound on his heart that had been very slow to heal – but his ready smile and quick wit were flashing out more often lately, and he seemed content with the decision he'd made last summer to leave the farm and retire to a quieter life. However, the seven grandchildren who were the light of his life were never far from his thoughts, and the reason for his frequent return visits to the farm.

Thomas had awoken that morning with no inkling of the tragedy that was already descending upon his family – a calamity that would change all their lives forever.

His day had started ordinarily enough – up early and eating breakfast in the kitchen as usual, reading the newspaper and making plans for the day, and generally enjoying his retirement in a neat little cottage in the heart of McLaren Vale. A large and fruitful vegetable garden kept Thomas busy, as did his prizewinning flock of Border Leicester ewes.

'Once a farmer always a farmer,' he supposed wryly; a true man of the land never retires completely.

Thomas's love of his adopted country ran very deep, and the small mementoes of his working life, the veggie garden and the sheep, kept him happy and fulfilled.

This peaceful existence was to be completely shattered when a loud knocking at the front door signaled the arrival of a telegraph marked 'Urgent.'

★

Four hours later found Thomas hunched in his seat in the otherwise empty compartment. Grey faced, and staring unseeing through the window at the dark, windswept landscape, he was the very picture of misery.

Bob, who had given up all hope of riding outside in the storm, had started weaving his way down the length of the rocking train, through the carriages, heading towards the guards van at the very rear.

Railway carriages of the day consisted of a long corridor with windows down one side, and five or six compartments with sliding doors and bench seats on the other. Ornate wooden panel work, shiny brass handles, and padded leather seats made the long hours of travel as comfortable as possible for the weary traveller, while the larger rural stations boasted well-equipped tearooms, at which a wide range of refreshments could be purchased.

Thomas however, could not have been less interested in refreshments or comfort. His burning desire was to reach Ucolta as quickly as possible, taking with him the vital parcel held so carefully in his lap.

His eyes closed, though he was far from sleep, and his thoughts drifted slowly back over the long years he'd spent working the farm. His had been a hard, wearying life, full of disappointments and sorrows, drought and flood; but it had not been without the joys of a bumper crop here and there, and a loving family, and the inner strength God gave him to get through the hard times.

Now his son Bill had taken over the acres out at Ucolta and, God willing, was carving out a decent life for Sarah and the children – he caught his breath. 'Oh dear Lord, those bonnie little kiddies!'

Rubbing his face with gnarly hands, he slumped back in his seat, staring blankly out of the window. Every now and then, he would fish the fateful telegraph out of his pocket and read it again. Even though every awful word was indelibly burned in his memory, he found it impossible to believe the truth of it.

'Father – come quickly – bring Diphtheria medicine – Mary Ann and Gilbert already gone to Our Lord – Sarah and rest of children gravely ill – no doctor here – please hurry Father – Bill.'

Hot tears blurred his vision, and he tucked the crumpled letter back into his coat pocket, shaking his head in sorrow as he remembered the two bright-eyed, happy little grandchildren he would never see again.

Sadly, things were only going to get worse for the McMurtrie family.

★

Bob, who was thinking only of the delights usually to be found in George Hiscock's lunch pail, was at this moment trotting past the open door of Thomas's compartment.

Now, as we all know, dogs are very special and intelligent animals, and will often be found sitting with people who are ill or unhappy. Their ability to comfort us in times of trouble is well known by every dog owner, and is undoubtedly the reason they are called 'man's best friend.'

Bob did a double-take as he passed the open doorway – the waves of pain and sorrow emanating from the compartment were enough to stop the little dog in his tracks. He stood for a moment, ears pricked and brow furrowed, unsure of what to do and swaying on his feet as the train lurched and rocked through the raging storm.

The old man's shoulders were slumped, his face ashen,

and his silver hair stood up every which way. In his lap was a small parcel wrapped in brown paper, and he kept at least one hand on this at all times. Now and then a tear would course its way down his cheek, and fall unchecked to the dusty carriage floor.

Bob's mind was made up. Putting all thoughts of George's lunch firmly to the back of his mind, he stepped quietly through the open door, and padded over to see what could be wrong. Feeling confident that one of his best cheery smiles would fix this problem quickly, Bob was surprised when the man did not even look at him. Not to be disheartened, Bob sat at the old man's feet and leaned against his legs. Hours passed, and the train ploughed steadily through the tempest – wind and rain lashed the carriage windows, and thunder cracked right overhead, deafening even over the racket of the train.

Small towns came and went – passengers disembarked, goods were unloaded – each stop an agony of time wasted for Thomas McMurtrie. He willed the train to go faster, but knew in his heart it would do no good – even if he were to arrive in Ucolta right now, he feared it would already be too late. As the train lumbered slowly into each station along the line, a small groan would escape his lips, and his knuckles showed white against the brown paper wrapping of his precious cargo.

Bob spent the entire journey through to Peterborough with the sad man, every now and then looking up at him with brow furrowed and head tilted to one side, very bewildered. The man gave little sign of having noticed the dog's presence, except once or twice when his hand came down and rested gently on Bob's head – just for a moment, but the comfort was mutual.

So, together like this, they finally pulled slowly into the busy hive of activity that was Peterborough Station. Darkness had fallen, and kerosene lanterns illuminated the platform in a soft yellow glow. The storm had been left behind near Hallett, but a cold wind wrapped icy fingers around those standing out on the platform.

Thomas stood up, his legs stiff and his back aching from the tension of the long journey. He looked down into two soft brown eyes peering quizzically up at him through a shaggy fringe, and tried to smile — this dog, though he'd never know it, had saved his sanity these past long hours. Bob showed him a crooked grin and offered his paw. The man leaned over stiffly, grasping the little foot for a brief moment before turning abruptly and staggering out of the carriage, wiping his eyes roughly with the back of his hand as he went.

★

A week had passed, and Bob had just returned from Sydney. He'd made the trip a few times over the past couple of years, and had many friends happy to accommodate him along the way. The cheerful barking from high atop the great steam engine as it hauled through towns and farmland became part of the rich history of the South Australian Railways. Children would hear the trains coming and run, hoping for a glimpse of the much talked about little dog.

On this particular morning, Bob was sitting on the platform at Peterborough Station. Before him was the most delightful of dilemmas. Should he jump on the next train down to Adelaide for a visit with his old friend Mr Evans, followed perhaps by a trip on the suburban line out to Port

Adelaide? This sounded very tempting, but there was also the express to Port Pirie leaving in an hour, which would give him time to share lunch with the men over in the goods shed. Yes, that was a better plan; his stomach was rumbling, and he could see the morning crew heading over to the sheds for their meal break. A small plume of smoke wafted up from behind the rough wooden buildings, which meant the billy was boiling and lunch was ready.

Confident of his welcome, Bob was trotting down the platform towards the rail yards, ears pricked and tongue lolling, as he happily pictured the delicious feast that was no doubt awaiting him – then all of a sudden his path was blocked by two large cardboard suitcases and a pair of black-clad legs.

Having to stop rather quickly, and with his mind completely focused on the imminent partaking of food; it took Bob a few moments to realise that the legs were very familiar – they should be, for he had studied them worriedly for many hours last week – they were the legs of the sad man.

Yes, it was Thomas McMurtrie. Exhausted and weighed down with sorrow, he was returning home to McLaren Vale after helping his son Bill to bury three more children and his beloved wife, Sarah. Just as he had dreaded, it had been too late to save them, even with the precious medicine he had carried so carefully all that way.

All that way, and yet too late.

Till the day he died, Thomas would never forget the sight of poor, broken-hearted Bill burying his much adored wife by the cold moonlight. The hurt, bewildered look on Bill's face, and the dreadful sounds of the first clods of earth hitting the top of the coffin would stay with him forever. Thomas had with him his two surviving granddaughters; they were pretty little girls, dressed in black with eyes downcast, they sat waiting with their hands folded quietly in their laps, attracting sympathetic looks and murmurs from the other travellers on the platform.

Thomas squatted down to greet Bob, having recognized him straight away.

That was the funny thing – the whole nightmare train trip last week was just a blur to him now, but he did remember clearly the scruffy brown dog who had sat with him the whole way, giving him a little extra courage in his hour of need.

Now, Bob obviously didn't understand what had happened to Thomas, or why he was so heavy-hearted, but he was very glad to see the old man again – the whipping tail, the crooked smile, and the little paw held up for a shake told Thomas he was remembered, and was now considered a friend.

The sharp whistle, announcing imminent departure, carried far up and down the platform. There were last-minute hugs and loading of bags, and the guard marched along the platform shutting the doors to each carriage and shouting, 'All Aboard!' to hurry people along.

Thomas was taking his two little granddaughters home to McLaren Vale for a few weeks while poor Bill had some time alone for mourning and prayer. Picking up the farm duties and starting life anew would come soon enough, but for now he just needed time by himself. His father had been dismayed, but also understanding of this decision, and had offered to care for young Edith and Jean until he was back on his feet. Thomas gathered up the little girls, and helped them to climb into the carriage, loading the bags up behind them. Leaning out of the window as the door shut behind him, Thomas could see Bob down on the platform, panting, looking up at him a little quizzically, but with his tail still waving and crooked teeth and pink tongue plain to see.

The train gave a jolt, and then started huff, huff, huffing its way slowly out of the station.

'Thankye, Laddie,' Thomas whispered, raising his hand in salute. 'Thankye.'

Bob watched the train until it disappeared from view, and then trotted down to the goods shed to see what the men were having for lunch.

CHAPTER TWELVE
AUGUST 1895

Old age had crept up quietly on Bob. His enthusiasm for travel and devotion to the trains never wavered, but as each year passed, he could feel himself slowing down more and more. The once strong little legs were aching most of the time now, and the fur around his muzzle had gradually turned from brown to grey. He also seemed to need a lot more sleep, and would often be found curled up in a quiet corner having a snooze.

All the station offices kept a box with a warm blanket ready by the fire for those times when Bob was in town, and the loco crews had all noticed the little dog walking stiffly and having a bit of trouble getting himself up into the trains. Of course, there was always a friendly pair of hands ready to help him up and down if needed, but mostly Bob was coping just fine on his own.

On the afternoon of Monday, the fifth of August, another bleak winter's day had settled in over the streets of Adelaide. Flat grey clouds blocked out the sun, leaving the sky overcast and dull, and the hurrying crowds were all warmly dressed in overcoats and hats. It had rained heavily that morning, and water splashed up over the kerb as the wheels of a horse-drawn tram churned through the puddles on the road.

Bob didn't care a jot! He was actually feeling quite sprightly today, and had almost entirely forgotten his various aches and pains. As he'd sat waiting on the footpath at the front of the butcher shop, he'd whiled away the time by barking loudly and happily at every trolley car that passed him by.

Mr Evans, as pleased as ever to see his old friend, presented Bob with a pork sausage and a large beef rissole, both of which were gratefully received, and quickly eaten! The old butcher gave Bob a quick rub on the cheek and then went back inside to his customers, some of whom could be seen frowning out through the shop window, annoyed to be kept waiting in favour of a mere dog.

A few drops of rain started to blow in on the choppy, ragged wind, parting Bob's fur and making him shiver. Suddenly, he didn't feel so well anymore.

At that moment, a strange thing happened.

A tall, rangy dog, jet black all over with a smooth, shiny, perfectly groomed coat, came trotting around the corner on the end of a short lead. On the other end of the lead was a beautiful lady in a long dress.

Bob didn't notice the lady – all he could see was the dog, who he hated on sight. He set up a frenzied barking and yodelling, telling the newcomer to back off and keep away from the butcher shop, which was Bob's private and exclusive territory.

The interloper pulled on his lead, hackles up and ready for a fight – he really was awfully big! Bob advanced towards him, quite enjoying the dust-up, but intent on seeing this dog off his street as quickly as possible.

Suddenly, Bob's irate barking broke off into an agonised yelp – and then silence.

Confused, he stood wavering for a moment on the footpath, the other dog forgotten as a bolt of excruciating pain shot through his body. A sharp whining cry, the last sound Bob would ever make, whistled through his crooked teeth. His legs, up til now so sturdy, gave way completely, and he slumped down onto the pavement.

Mr Evans, who had witnessed the whole event through his shop window, was absolutely horrified. He rushed outside, still wearing his apron and paper hat, and hurried over to the quiet little figure lying oh-so-still on the hard footpath.

'Bob! Bob!' he called in a shaky voice.

Bob didn't move.

A small crowd had started to gather round, although the elegant woman and her dog had disappeared fairly quickly – she certainly wasn't going to trouble herself over the life and death of a homeless waif.

★

Mr Evans knelt down beside the little body and called his name once more. Bob could hear the pleading voice of his oldest friend, but it was very faint, and seemed to come from far, far away. The noisy bustle of the street faded away. He could feel the gentle hands of the butcher stroking his fur as the spinning world around him went quiet and it became very dark. Bob was not afraid. He felt no pain; he could see nothing, hear nothing, feel nothing. It seemed to be dark and quiet for a long, long time.

Finally, very faintly, a sound came to him – a comforting, homely sound – the early morning warbling of a lone magpie. The song grew louder, and closer, and was soon joined by the excited chatterings of a distant flock of galahs, carefree and happy as they flew high above, through an endless perfect sky.

As if in a dream (although Bob knew this was too real to be a dream), the clean, rich scent of the hills and sweeping vistas of home filled his heart, and suddenly there it was – the shrill whistle of the 5.20 Special rumbling down out of the hills towards Peterborough, the chugging and huffing getting louder and louder, the thrilling smells of coal and steam filling the air…

With a deep sense of peace and comfort, Bob knew that he had come home, where he was always meant to be – the place Bob loved and where he was loved, the place he had returned to and now would never leave.

★

Mr Evans sat on the kerb with Bob's head in his lap, smoothing the rough grey and brown fur around the dog's face with shaking hands. He knew there was quite a crowd gathered around, he could hear their concerned murmurings and felt a couple of sympathetic pats on his shoulder, but the poor man was quite unable to move. Mr Evans was shocked and heartbroken. This had all happened so quickly. His blurry, tear-filled eyes spoke volumes; his sorrow was deeper than he would have thought possible – and all over a dog?

'Yes' he thought. 'Bugger it, a bloody one in a million dog, and one of the best friends a chap could 'ave. I s'pose 'is poor liddle heart must 'ave jus' wore itself out.'

Wiping his face roughly with his hanky, the old man clambered stiffly to his feet and then ever-so-gently lifted the little body up from the cold pavement and carried it round to the yard at the rear of the shop.

He laid Bob carefully on an old table under the verandah, and spent a few minutes checking the already dull eyes and feeling the furry chest just to be absolutely sure. Alas, it was certain. The once bright little face was now quiet in death, and the finality of this made Mr Evans well up all over again.

★

Two grave, quiet men from Adelaide Station came to the butcher's yard later that evening and took Bob's body away, and that was the end – well, almost the end of the story.

Word of Bob's death spread quickly around the state. The enigmatic brown dog had made many friends in his years riding the rails, and had left an indelible impression even on those whose lives he had just passed through.

It had never really occurred to anyone that Bob might grow old and die. 'Bob the Railway Dog' had been such a regular part of life in the mid-north, everyone felt that they knew him – so the news came as a real shock to many, many people.

Of course, it didn't take too long for word to reach Will Ferry in Western Australia. Harold had telegraphed him pretty well straight away, not wanting Mary to hear it from anyone else.

William knew he would have to tell her immediately. He got straight up out of his chair in the station office and walked home, worried about how on earth he was going to break this news to his dear wife. Leaving Bob behind in Peterborough had been heartbreaking for Mary, even though they had known full well that the dog's happiness depended on it.

As it was, Mary took one look at William's face as he walked in the back door, and knew it was bad news. 'It's Bob, dear.' he said.

She pulled out one of the wooden kitchen chairs and sat at the table as William held her hand and filled her in on the details. Mary didn't say much, just gulped a few times and clutched her hanky, accepting the inevitable.

Thoughts of Bob weighed heavily on her mind for days, and Mary found herself either smiling or wiping her eyes as her heart overflowed with memories of the plucky, bright eyed little dog.

A few days after Bob's death, *The Advertiser* newspaper published a lengthy obituary on him, rich with stories and anecdotes of his life and times. Mary cut these out and pasted them into a book.

As the weeks and months, and even years, went by articles and stories continued to appear occasionally in local papers. People did not forget Bob, and stories of his exploits were re-lived over dinner tables and in hotel bars, station tearooms, railway barracks and bunkhouses all over the country for many years to come.

As Mary and William had often said – they'd known right from the very first day there was something special about him.

'Goodbye Bob – Goodbye.'

THE END

Home keeping dogs have homely wits, their notions tame and poor.
I scorn the dog who humbly sits before the cottage door.
Or those who weary vigils keep, or follow lowly kine.
A dreary life midst stupid sheep shall ne'er be lot of mine.
For free from thrall I travel far, no 'fixed abode' I own;
I leap aboard a railway car, by everyone I'm known.
Today I'm here; tomorrow brings scenes miles and miles away.
Born swiftly on steams rushing wings, I see fresh friends each day.
Each driver from the footplate hails my coming with delight,
Again from all upon the rails, a welcome ever bright.
I share the perils of the line with mates from end to end,
Who would not for all a silver mine, have harm befall their friend.
Then other dogs may snarl and fight, round city purlieus prowl;
Or render hideous the night with unmelodious howl.
I have a cheery bark for all, no ties my travels clog,
I hear the whistle – that's the call, for Bob the driver's dog.

Anon.

ACKNOWLEDGEMENTS

Heather Parker: *Historian, Peterborough History Group*
John Mannion: *Historian, Peterborough History Group*
Alison Dunling: *Curator, Terowie Museum*
Bill Giddings: *Tour Guide, Peterborough Steamtown*
Doug Perrot: *Tour Guide, Peterborough Steamtown*
The National Railway Museum, Port Adelaide
Staff of the State Library of South Australia

Bob statue – Main St, Peterborough

BIBLIOGRAPHY

Deceptive Lands by Roma Mattey

Hear The Other Side by Wallace B Budd

Petersburg To Peterborough by Anita Woods

I Remember Mount Mary by Margaret Zerner

Glimpses Of The North East by Gladys Ward

Curiosities Of South Australia by Russell Smith

Narrow Gauge Memories – The Personalities by Kenn Pearce

Peterborough 125 by Steve McNicol

An article, taken from the Historical Society of SA newsletter, written by Geoffrey H Manning

ABOUT THE AUTHOR

The author holds a deep and lifelong affection for the South Australian mid-north, and particularly the town of Peterborough – her grandparents ran the Peterborough Hotel during the 1960s, and many happy childhood memories of a thriving railway town still remain.

The discovery of a portrait of the enigmatic 'Bob the Railway Dog' was the inspiration for this book, and the author hopes it is a fitting tribute to a wonderful Australian character and the community he loved.

ORDER

	QTY
The Railway Dog $24.99	....
Postage within Australia (1 book) $5.00	....
Postage within Australia (2 or more books) $9.00	....

TOTAL* $_____

* All prices include GST

Name: ....

Address: ....

....

Phone: ....

Email Address: ....

Payment:

❏ Money Order ❏ Cheque ❏ Amex ❏ MasterCard ❏ Visa

Cardholder's Name:..

Credit Card Number: ....

Signature:..

Expiry Date: ....

Allow 21 days for delivery.

BE PUBLISHED

Publishing through a successful Australian publisher. Brolga provides:
- Editorial appraisal
- Cover design
- Typesetting
- Printing
- Author promotion
- National book trade distribution, including sales, marketing and distribution through Simon & Schuster Australia & New Zealand.

For details and inquiries, contact:
Brolga Publishing Pty Ltd
PO BOX 452
Torquay 3228 Victoria.

bepublished@brolgapublishing.com.au
markzocchi@brolgapublishing.com.au
ABN: 46 063 962 443